KRISTOPHER RUFTY

This book is a work of fiction. The names, characters, places, and incidents are products of the writer's imagination or have been used fictitiously and are not to be construed as real. Any resemblance to persons, living or dead, actual events, locale or organizations is entirely coincidental.

Machete Mama
Paperback Edition
Copyright © 2025 Kristopher Rufty
Edited by 360 Editing (a division of Uncomfortably Dark Horror).
Editor: Candace Nola
Cover Design: D.A. Design Copyright © 2025

All Rights Are Reserved. No part of this book may be used or reproduced in any manner whatsoever without written permission, except in the case of brief quotations embodied in critical articles and reviews.

ISBN 9798312677652

DEDICATION

For Cynthia Rothrock.

Penny Chambers pulled up to the gas pump, almost crying out in victory. Putting her Jeep in park, she shut off the engine. "Made it," she said.

Anna looked up from her phone. It might have been the first time her neck had been erect in over two hours. "Huh?" Squinting as she looked around, she said, "Where are we?"

"The moon," said Penny, laughing. "Where do you think?"

Anna rolled her eyes. Penny wondered if that was how she'd looked at seventeen during the many occasions she'd rolled her own eyes because of something an adult said.

I'd like to think I was as pretty as Anna.

But Penny found that hard to believe. Sure, she'd been a pretty girl growing up and still was easy on the eyes, she knew. Enough unwanted attention always came her way from obnoxious guys who thought they were all she'd ever wanted. Anna had inherited all of that, plus the good looks from their father.

"I hope the moon has a toilet," said Anna. "My back teeth are floating."

"Nice image," said Penny. "Restroom's inside."

The gas station doubled as a truck stop. On the other side of the large building were countless semi-trucks parked throughout a grassy field, while others were sitting next to gas pumps.

Anna flung the blanket she'd been snuggling with aside. Her bare legs stretched out in front of her while she arched her back, bringing her bent arms up so her hands were beside her face. She let out a long moan as she twitched.

The noises she made were enough to wake up Ashley in the backseat. Penny's oldest daughter sat up, her face blank as she looked around. "What the hell?" said Ashley.

"Language," said Penny, digging for her wallet in her pocketbook.

Ignoring her, Ashley said, "Where are we?"

"The moon," said Anna. "Didn't you read the sign when we landed?"

"Stealing my jokes," muttered Penny.

Ashley leaned forward, putting her head between the seats as she studied the gas station. "Oh, I know where we are. Didn't we stop here last time we came out this way?"

"You remember that? You were three years old!" How Ashley remembered almost every detail of every situation amazed Penny. Especially now since it had been so long since they'd been in these mountains.

Anna rolled those big eyes again. "You probably remember the night you were conceived."

"No," said Ashley, "but I remember the night *you* were." Laughing, Ashley climbed out.

Penny felt heat in her cheeks. She looked over at Anna, smiled. "I'm sure she's joking."

Another eye roll. "Gross." Anna opened the door and slid out of the Jeep.

Penny got out next. The air outside was muggy and smelled like stale gasoline. The sounds of cars zipping along carried over from the interstate, blending with the song coming from the speakers mounted on the tin canopy above them.

She stood beside the car while her daughters made their way around to the front. Penny realized they were still wearing the clothes they'd slept in the night before: loose T-shirts and tight shorts that were very short, barely covering the curves of their rumps. She thought about telling them to get their lounge pants out of the car but knew they would protest. Besides, no matter how much she hated it, they weren't little girls anymore. Besides, men would stare at them in anything they wore. Ashley was a sophomore in college, and Anna would be starting her senior year in high school in August. Somehow, her little girls had grown up.

"You all right, Mom?"

Penny blinked. She turned and saw Ashley looking at her as if she'd accidentally farted. Smiling, she said, "I'm fine. Just spacing out."

"Want me to take over driving? You've done it this whole time."

"Nah, I'll be okay. We don't have much further to go."

Ashley didn't look as if she believed her. But she only said, "Okay."

"Come on," said Anna. "I have to *pee.*"

"Subtle, isn't she?" said Ashley.

"I'll be in there in a few," said Penny."

Ashley and Anna had already turned away from her and were heading toward the gas station. Daylight was fading behind the building, spilling thick pink syrup across the sky. It had been a long time since she'd seen a sunset out here.

She'd wanted to get to the cabin before dark. They weren't going to make it. That was fine. They could get the essentials unloaded from the car and just take it easy tonight. Start everything else tomorrow.

Penny swiped her card and inserted the nozzle into the tank. She pulled back the lever, flipping the switch so it would stay on. She hated leaving it pumping unattended like this, but she needed to visit the restroom just as much the girls did.

Penny used the key remote to lock the doors and made her way inside the gas station. From the dimming light outside, the brightness of the store made her squint. The air conditioning felt good. She sighed as she searched the store for the restrooms.

Ashley probably remembers where it is.

"Looking for the restroom?"

Penny turned toward the register. A short, plump woman stood behind the counter, bagging some snacks for an older man who didn't turn to look at her.

Smiling, Penny nodded. "That obvious, huh?"

The woman pointed over her shoulder. "That way."

"Thanks," said Penny.

She made her way around the counter, stepping between other customers. She noticed how they watched her, but pretended as if she were oblivious to their stares.

Penny spotted the *Restroom* sign extending from the wall. A doorway led into a small foyer where a water fountain separated two doors. The women's restroom was on the left. As she approached, the women's door flung open. Anna stepped out first, drying her hands with a paper towel. Ashley was right behind her.

Penny felt relieved seeing them.

Anna smiled, then patted Penny's shoulder. "Have fun in there."

Ashley made a face. "We'll meet you outside."

"Want anything, go ahead and grab it," said Penny.

"We're good," said Ashley.

Penny entered the restroom. It smelled like a combination of bleach and garbage. The hollow sounds of water dripping echoed as if she were standing in a cave. A trash can was in the corner, under the hand dryer and paper towel dispenser. It was overflowing with wadded paper. A pile had gathered around the can. On her way to the nearest stall, she passed messages written on the walls in marker and lipstick.

A few minutes later, Penny was finished. She dried her hands, then used the paper towel as a glove on the handle to open the door.

It was brighter in the main area than the restroom. She was heading to the door when she heard somebody say, "Penny?"

The voice sounded familiar. Older, more mature than when she'd last heard it, but she knew it. Penny turned around. A woman her age stared back at her. Pretty and blond, her face was tanned and smooth, with eyes that looked like crystals, though her age showed in the creases. When she smiled, she seemed to revert to the youthful form of Penny's memory.

"Misty?" she said.

"It's me," said Misty, laughing. She stepped forward, opening her arms. "It's been so long!"

"It really has!"

They hugged. Misty was taller than her, slim, but with curves where they mattered to those who looked. When they were teenagers, other kids used to comment how odd it was the tallest girl and shortest girl in class were best friends.

"What is that?" said Misty, easing out of the hug. She reached out and gently gripped Penny's biceps. "Damn girl. You must still hit the gym pretty hard. Do you still train like you did for the movies?" She held up her hand, fingers flat and straight as if chopping the air.

"Well..." Penny shrugged. She felt herself blush. She didn't really want to get into her training routine in the gas station with other customers watching. "What have you been up to these days?"

Misty smiled. "What can I be up to out here?" Laughing, she aimed her thumb over her shoulder at the patrons. "I own the daycare most of their kids attend."

"Oh, wow! That's so great. You always wanted to work with kids."

A flash of sadness showed in Misty's eyes, but it was quickly gone. Not quick enough, though, because Penny saw it. "That's true. Been running the daycare for almost twenty years now."

"Wow, that's great. A long time. You still live in the same place?"

"Yeah. All by my lonesome. How about you? What are you doing these days?"

"Kind of figuring that out at the moment."

"I heard you retired from the movie business. That true?"

Though she no longer lived here, the small town somehow still knew all about her. "Not exactly. Just kind of...weighing options."

"Are you going to stay in the cabin?"

Penny nodded. "That's why we're out here. I was left the whole estate."

"I'm sorry about your aunt. She was really a…" Misty frowned as if lost in thought.

"A bitch," said Penny. "I know."

Misty's cheeks flushed red. "I wasn't going to say *that*. But now that you mention it. Wait—you said 'we.'"

"I did. My daughters are with me."

"You have more than one girl now?"

"Two girls. It's been a long time since I've been out here."

"It really has. Their ages?"

"Practically grown. They're…"

Penny turned to point at her car through the glass doors to show Misty. She'd expected to see the girls standing around the car, waiting for her to return. Instead, she spotted them just outside, blocked by a small group of young men that had intercepted them on their way through the parking lot. Ashley stood partway in front of her younger sister, head turning while staying focused on their fans.

"Shit,' said Penny.

"What is it?" said Misty, looking. She saw the gathering outside, and her dusky face seemed to blanch even more. "Damn it."

2

Without another word, Penny started walking. The doors whirred open as she approached. Anna looked over her shoulder, saw her mother, and sighed as relief washed over her. "Mom!"

Ashley turned around, looking just as reassured.

"Uh-oh, Levi, Mama's here."

Penny wasn't sure who had said that, but she could tell who Levi was from the way he turned to acknowledge the statement. He was dressed in a flannel shirt, the sleeves cut off to show his muscular arms. He had some tribal sleeves tattooed on his skin.

Penny didn't want any trouble, especially so soon. She hadn't even been to the cabin yet. Her plan had been to slip in and out without many people realizing she'd come through. In the few minutes she'd been here, she had already bumped into her childhood friend, and now the girls had walked into another situation.

The kind of altercation this scene could lead to was something she didn't need. Yet, she somehow knew it was going to happen, regardless of her intentions. She might have even known before leaving their house in Georgia.

"Come on, girls," said Penny. "Time for us to go. Tell your friends, 'Bye.'"

Penny started to walk toward the car, but the group of boys moved to the right to block her. Penny counted four of them, all around the same age. No older than twenty-five, any of them.

"Where you runnin' off to?" said Levi, stepping directly in front of her. He was easily a foot taller than her and wider on both sides. She could smell liquor in his breath, blending with the heavy tang of his cologne. A good-looking boy that would probably be gorgeous if he wasn't so disgusting.

"Got somewhere to be?" asked a shorter guy behind Levi. His hair was closely cropped to his head, as if he'd just come from the military.

"Yes, we do," said Penny. "Come on, girls."

Anna and Ashley made no attempt to move.

"They won't let us," said Anna.

The boys laughed. Somebody mimicked Anna in a squeaky voice.

"Yes, they will," said Penny. "I'm sure these are good boys that don't want any trouble."

More laughter.

Then Levi said, "I think they want to stay. What do you think, Tommy?"

The buzz-cut kid nodded. "I think so."

The two quiet ones smiled, gave each other fist bumps.

Levi turned to Penny again, smirking. His eyes looked her up and down. She could feel them peeling away her clothes to see underneath. He must have conjured a pleasurable visual because his teeth clamped down on his bottom lip. "Damn, Mama," he said, eyes locked on her breasts. "I see where the girls get their looks from. But that body is all *you*. Look at them *tits*. I bet they're real, ain't they? You didn't pay for them. No way in hell did you pay for those."

She was wearing a shirt with a wide neck that showed a pond of skin and the two slopes of her breasts. There was no hiding them from his leering gaze.

Heat flowed through Penny. Not the kind that came from a sweet compliment that she wouldn't know how to react to. This was a burn that was very familiar, a feeling caused by anger.

Penny looked him in the eye. "A gift from God."

Levi laughed. "Damn right, Mama. And don't God say you supposed to share with your neighbor or some shit?" He looked at Tommy. "Right?"

Nodding, Tommy said, "Treat them as yourself."

"Right," said Levi. He brought his focus back to Penny. "Treat me like you'd treat you. I know *you* get to touch them. Probably a lot, since they're on your body. I mean, you have to look at them every day and wonder how in the hell you got so lucky with a pair like that. I bet them nipples are like little dots *until* they're messed with. Then they probably get hard like nails." He let out a honking laugh that triggered laughter from his pals.

"Pig," said Anna, her teeth clenched.

Be quiet, Anna.

Penny almost reached out and covered her daughter's mouth. There was still a chance they could get through this without anything else happening.

Levi threw back his head and let out a wild guffaw. Then he started snorting. Nose wrinkled, lips puckered, he snorted over and over.

Penny wondered why nobody had tried to intervene. She saw people scattered throughout the parking lot, standing by their cars, observing, and doing nothing. Penny wasn't too surprised, though. Most people pretended as if they couldn't see something bad was happening, even if it were right in front of them. A group of guys like these assholes would intimidate almost anyone.

Almost.

Penny wasn't one of those people. All these boys were doing was pissing her off.

Levi stopped snorting, then faced Penny again. His eyes slipped downward to stare at her chest. He whistled.

"Don't do what you're thinking," said Penny. She spoke slowly, with just a hint of gravity in her voice. She never took her eyes away from Levi's. "Just don't."

"You know what I'm thinking?"

"I do. You're not the first to ever think it."

"I bet not," he said. "When you look like that, I bet I'm just a name on a long list. But I'm probably the best-looking. Am I right?"

"Not even close, pal."

Levi's smirk returned. He rubbed his chin. "That doesn't bother me a bit."

Penny saw his hand reach out. She could have caught it right there, but she needed him to make contact first. If he didn't, then the boys could say she attacked him. Didn't really matter if he was provoking her or not, she needed him to make the first *physical* move.

His hand slipped past the wide neckline of her shirt. His beefy fingers cupped her left breast.

That was just what she needed.

"You really messed up," said Anna.

Levi started to open his mouth, to either say something stupid, or to ask Anna to elaborate. He didn't have the chance. Because when he started to turn his head, Penny shifted her weight to her right foot, jumped onto her left and brought her right foot up in one quick motion.

The toes of her shoe connected under Levi's chin, throwing back his head. His hand flew out of her shirt as his body tilted back. Both feet lifted in the air, dropping him. He hit the concrete sprawling just as Penny landed in a position that made it look as if she hadn't moved at all.

She noticed only two of the guys staring down at Levi, the two quiet ones. She didn't see Tommy anywhere. Then she noticed a flicker of movement off to her right, almost hidden behind the curtain of her long hair. The blur was coming at her fast.

Just not fast enough.

She stepped back, spun around with her leg fully extended. Her timing had been perfect, and she caught Tommy in the gut, folding him over her leg as the air blasted from his mouth. Before he could even try to breathe, Penny was already swinging up with a forearm, clocking him on the jaw.

He landed beside Levi, who was just starting to stir again.

Anna pointed at the remaining guys. "Ha *ha!* That's right! Our mom knows how to kick ass!"

Ashley shook her head. "She warned you. She really did. She warned you."

Penny remained in her fighting stance, daring the other two to try something. They looked as if they might be tempted, but so far, they hadn't made any kind of move that would suggest they were dumb enough to try.

Penny kind of hoped they would, though. It would be harder to take on two at once, but she didn't doubt she could do it. No way were these assholes trained in anything other than beer and fart jokes.

"Damn, Penny Duvall. You're just as spunky as you ever were."

Another familiar voice, same gruff drawl, but now with age and whiskey added to it. Penny glanced over her shoulder and saw first the shiny star pinned on a tanned uniform shirt. Then she saw the squinted eyes, mouth curved into a smile to show nice teeth. A few days' worth of stubble brushed his cheeks. His head was shaved down to a bristly layer. When she'd seen him last, he'd still let his hair grow out.

"Charlie Barger," said Penny, smiling.

"*Sheriff* Barger," he said.

"And I'm Penny *Chambers* now."

"Ah," he said, shaking his head. Approaching her, he added, "Do I need to draw my gun?"

"On me?" she said.

"On them," he nodded toward the other two, still standing. "Or should I just sit back and watch?"

Penny let out a breath. She relaxed her arms, then brushed the loose hair away from her face. "How you been, Charlie?"

"Not bad. What'd these shits do to deserve what you gave them?"

"Levi there got a little touchy."

"He does that."

"And Tommy tried to get me from behind."

"Looks like you got him, though."

"I warned them."

"I bet you did." He laughed. "They're too young to remember your ass-kicking movies."

"A lot of people are."

"Want to press charges?"

Penny shrugged. "I guess not."

Smiling, Charlie said, "They'll have to live with the ribbing they'll get from everybody in town."

"That's probably punishment enough."

Charlie nodded. Then he looked at the other two, standing there as if they didn't know what they should do. "Get these sacks of shit and get out of here."

Nodding, they each grabbed one under their arms, turned, and hurried away, dragging the other two. They reached a big truck with wheels almost as tall as Penny's Jeep. Opening the tailgate, they helped Levi and Tommy into the back. Once they were in, they shut the tailgate, piled into the front, and drove away.

"Problem solved," said Charlie.

"Thanks," said Penny.

"Glad I could help by doing nothing at all."

Penny smiled. "You look good in the uniform."

"Well, I guess that's something. Walk me to my car?" He gestured toward the SUV parked in a space near the left side of the building. *Sheriff* adorned the door above a large gold star. A light rack was on top.

"Sure," she said. She turned to the girls, holding out the keys. "Head to the car. I'll be there in a minute."

Ashley and Anna looked at her, fighting back the grins that tugged at their mouths.

"He's an old friend from school."

"Right," said Anna, taking the keys.

"It's true," said Charlie. "Friends. Your mother wouldn't date me, no matter how much I begged."

"You hardly ever begged."

"I guess we have different ideas of begging."

Penny laughed.

"Not even going to introduce us," said Ashley. "Rude."

"Sorry. Charlie—Sheriff, this is Ashley and Anna. My girls."

"They look just like you."

"That's good for us," said Anna.

"Good for a lot of people," said Charlie, winking.

Anna's cheeks reddened.

"Come on," said Ashley, pulling her sister. "Let's give them their privacy."

Charlie laughed. "Nice to meet you, girls."

"You, too!" said Ashley without looking back.

They watched them until they reached the car, then Charlie turned to her. "Shall we?"

"Sure."

They started toward the SUV, moving slowly. "Heading to your aunt's cabin?"

Penny nodded. "I guess everybody knows. I was trying to do it quietly."

"This is Briarwood, North Carolina. You can't do anything quietly here."

"One thing I always hated about this place."

Charlie nodded. "It never seemed like the town was a good fit for you."

"Maybe I wasn't a good fit for the town."

Charlie shrugged. "I heard your aunt left everything to you."

"I was surprised. We didn't really get along."

"You're her only family."

"I know. But she said she was going to leave it to the state or anybody other than me."

"She left you everything, then?"

"She did."

"Planning to move back? Sell it?"

Penny didn't feel comfortable talking about this, even to Charlie. Sure, he was somewhat of an acquaintance from the past, but it was still her private business.

Then she remembered Misty. Looking over her shoulder at the store, she tried to spot her old friend through the glass. She didn't see her anywhere.

"Everything okay?"

"Huh?" Penny looked at Charlie. "Oh, yes. Fine. How long have you been the sheriff?"

"Too long," he said, laughing softly.

"That's good, though. You're doing good things."

"I wish."

"What do you mean?"

Charlie shrugged. "Briarwood isn't the same town it was when we were kids."

"What town is?"

"True. But this one *really* isn't. Being this far out in the hills, with nothing much to do, lots of folks turned to cooking meth or getting into some hell or the other. To be such a small town, it keeps me pretty damn busy, like it was a big city that only pays me the small-town bucks."

"Well, you have a police force, right?"

"Sure. A small one. They do what they can."

"That's all anybody can expect."

"Come on, Penny. You know that's not how it works. These people expect us to wipe out all the crime and get Briarwood back to the way it used to be when their grandparents were young. The more trash I clean out of here, even more moves in. A damn shit cycle that never ends."

Penny felt sad listening to him talk. She'd grown up here, sure, but she never felt as if she had any roots here. Her aunt had raised her after her parents were killed in a car crash when she was four. But her aunt had never really spent much time trying to understand Penny. They were just two people in a house, and Penny just happened to be a minor most of the time. Soon as she was eighteen, she'd headed for California and had only been back a few times.

"So, anyway, welcome home." Charlie put on a big smile as he stepped over to his police-issued wheels.

"Oh, thanks. I feel so good about it now."

"Just giving you the heads up, is all. Overall, the town is fine. Just got to know what to look out for. But after seeing what you did, I think you already have an eye for it."

"For?"

"Trouble. Finding it and getting into it."

Penny shrugged. She smiled. "I do what *I* can."

"Right. So that's really you kicking all that ass in those movies? Not a stunt person?"

"I do my own stunts."

"Fancy. Could you do that back in school?"

"No way. You saw how I was in school. Mousey, my nose in books."

"That's not what I saw back then."

Now it was Penny's turn to blush. She could feel a different kind of heat in her cheeks, but hoped it was too dark for Charlie to notice.

"But seriously, that was some impressive skills. I was all prepared to step in, but you had it handled before I even got out of the car."

"Thanks. I take the craft very seriously."

"It shows. Maybe you'll tell me about it one day. How you got into those martial arts flicks and stuff."

"Maybe."

"Be careful driving out there. It's damn dark on those roads at night."

"I remember."

Penny wiggled her fingers in a wave, then turned away. She could feel Charlie's eyes on her. She remembered how back in school he'd tried to get her to date him many times. He hadn't been exaggerating about that with the girls. She'd tutored him in English and Literature and had spent a lot of time at his house. Not once had they even kissed, though Charlie had tried multiple times.

Why didn't I ever give him a chance?

She knew why. He made her feel uncomfortable. He always had. Even now, knowing he was watching her, caused a cold tendril to work its way up her spine. She got that way with most men, though. Not all of them would go as far as Levi did and force himself on her. But she could usually tell when they wanted to.

Not Alex.

No, not him. He was the exception to the paranoid fear she had about men. He'd been good. Amazing.

Amazing Alex.

Her throat felt tight. She pushed away thoughts of the girls' father. For now. Later, with wine, she would let them come. And she would also let the tears that usually accompanied them reach her as well.

"There it is!" Ashley said, her voice loud in the car.

Anna, behind the wheel, let out a squeak and stomped the brakes. The tires made scratchy sounds as they skidded over the gravel. Clouds of dust swirled up into the path of the headlights and climbed the windows like churning gray water.

"Damn it, Ash," said Anna. "You scared the shit out of me!"

"Well, you were about to pass it! I told you I should've drove!"

Penny, turning in the passenger seat so she could see both girls, said, "Anna, language. Ashely, stop yelling."

Both girls nodded but said nothing.

"You're doing fine," Penny told Anna. "Just turn the wheel sharper and you should be fine."

"Fine for what?"

"To get in the driveway."

Anna shoved her fingers into her hair, pulling it away from her face and holding it there. "I almost took out the mailbox."

Penny noted that the front end of the car was pretty close to the mailbox standing on the right side of the driveway. On the side, the numbers 285 were faded. "It's fine. Just turn the wheel far as you can. It'll be easier than trying to back up on this road. You might drive off the side, and if we end up in the gulley, we're stuck."

"No pressure," Anna muttered, turning the wheel.

"You'll be all right," said Ashley.

"No thanks to you."

"Enough," said Penny. She knew the girls were tired of being cooped up in the car. It had been a long day, with an unexpectedly chaotic event at the gas station. They were ready to unwind. Penny had to admit she was ready as well. The bottle of wine she'd brought was calling her.

Though Anna groaned and made squeaky noises while doing so, she had no problem steering the car into the driveway. She kept it slow as she headed into the woods. The trees on either side of the driveway blocked out the moonlight, making it look as if they were driving through a woodsy tunnel.

When they exited the conduit of trees, the yard spread out on all sides. The cabin sat on the left, a pale shape under the silver light. All the windows were dark. There were no outside lights on, no safety lights. Only the stars and moon and headlights offered any type of luminosity.

"Is the power on?" asked Ashley.

"It's supposed to be," said Penny. "I called them a few days ago and paid to have it switched over."

"Looks like a tomb," said Anna.

"Great," said Ashley.

"Maybe some vampires have shacked up in there. Bloodsucking squatters."

"Very funny," said Penny.

Anna parked next to the cabin. The headlights cut through the darkness, highlighting the shed near the edge of the yard. Beyond it was a barrier of trees squeezed close together. In the far distance, she could see the jagged black shapes of mountains against the starry backdrop.

Penny had always adored the seclusion this place offered. Right now, though, it felt as if they were alone in the world. Maybe that wasn't such a bad thing.

Felt unnatural, though, and Penny didn't like that.

It's just being here again. That's the problem.

"Let's get inside first," said Penny. "We'll come back out for the bags once we get some lights on."

Anna reached for the keys to turn off the car.

"Leave the lights on," said Penny.

Nodding, Anna twisted the keys. The engine puttered into silence. The steady drone of crickets and frogs faded in. Every so often, an owl chimed in.

"Sounds like the bugs are screaming," said Ashley. She opened the back door. The dome light clicked on, spreading light through the cab.

Squinting at the weak brightness, Penny laughed. "Better than traffic noise."

"Just barely," said Anna.

They climbed out of the car. Penny dug out the small manilla envelope the lawyer had given her this morning. She shook it. She could feel the two keys scraping against the paper.

"Well," said Ashley. "Are we going in?"

Nodding, Penny tried to put on a good smile. She suddenly felt nervous. "Let's go."

Penny started walking. The girls followed closely behind. The headlights shining behind them caused their shadows to stretch across the front porch. Where it wrapped around the side of the cabin was brimming with darkness. At one time, her aunt had kept plants hanging in pots all around the porch. She could tell it was devoid of all plant life now.

Reaching the front door, Penny tore open the envelope she'd received from the lawyer's office. She shook out a single key into her palm. "Hopefully he gave us the right key."

"It's probably one key for all the locks," said Ashley.

"Let's hope," said Penny.

Turned out, Ashley was right. The one key unlocked both the deadbolt and doorknob. Penny swung the door open. Light from the headlights spilled into the deep blackness filling the cabin. The silence was heavy with the fusty air.

"The A/C wasn't cut on," said Anna. "I thought you told them to have it on."

"I did," said Penny.

Penny walked deeper into the cabin. She turned, spotting the girls still standing by the doorway. "Come on," she said.

"Nuh uh," said Anna. "Not until you get some lights on. That's horror movie darkness in there."

"Good grief," muttered Penny. Though she had to admit, she felt a little spooked herself by how dark and quiet it was inside. She made her way along the wall, hand sliding across until her fingers brushed the jutting tips of light switches. She was surprised she still remembered where they were. "Found the lights. Here's hoping they work."

She flipped the switches.

Light blasted all the darkness away.

"And God said let there be light," said Ashley.

"Ash," said Penny.

"Sorry."

The light on the porch was working now, so Penny assumed the safety light on the side probably had turned on as well.

"Let's get it done," she said.

They managed to finish unloading the car in only a couple back and forth trips. The cooler was last, and Penny let the girls tag team that one.

"Leave it on the porch," she told them. "Just bring in the stuff that needs to go in the fridge."

"And the Pepsi," said Ashley.

And my wine.

The girls transferred the important contents from the cooler to the kitchen. While they took their bags upstairs to choose their rooms for the next few days, Penny stayed downstairs, making sandwiches for them. She'd rather have pizza, but being this late in the evening and so far out in the woods, she doubted anybody would deliver. And she did *not* feel like driving into town to pick up one.

Should've thought of it sooner.

Sandwiches would be fine, though. Turkey and ham. She used the rest of the tomatoes she'd sliced before they left, topping the sandwiches with shredded lettuce. There were cucumbers and broccoli left as well, so she put them on the side of the paper plates. They'd eaten this same meal twice already today, but one more time wouldn't hurt.

It felt awkward to call out for the girls in a strange house, so she sent a text to tell them the food was ready. Within a couple seconds of her sending the message, she heard the stomps of their feet as they rushed to the stairs. Their footfalls turned to hollow bangs on their way down.

Anna hurried into the kitchen first. For a brief moment, she was a little girl again, hurrying to beat her bigger sister at any race they could come up with. The image of her youngest daughter, smaller with big eyes and an even bigger smile, dissolved and reverted back to her teenaged self. Much more beautiful, with the same big eyes, though filled with knowledge that they hadn't possessed at her younger age.

"You okay, Mom?" asked Anna.

Penny blinked. She smiled. "Fine. Grab a plate. Let's eat in the dining room."

"Dining room? Fancy."

"*We* have a dining room."

"Yeah, but you use it as your office."

Penny nodded. "That's true. I'm probably going to use this one also when I write later."

Ashley came into the kitchen. On her way to the fridge, she said, "I'll grab us some drinks."

"I'll take some of that wine Mom's planning on drinking later," said Anna.

"Like hell," said Penny. "Go through there." She nodded toward the doorway on the far side of the kitchen. It was a block of darkness that began where the kitchen floor ended.

"Eh, you first," she said.

Laughing softly, Penny walked to the doorway. Holding her plate in one hand, she reached into the black with the other. She found the light switch and flipped it on. Light popped in the room, bouncing off the glossy surface of the dining table. Though it shone, under the chandelier Penny could see a light layer of dust covering it.

"Better?" Penny asked.

Nodding, Anna entered the dining room. She put her plate at the spot to the right. Penny followed her, placing her plate at the head of the table and Ashley's across from Anna. Ashley joined them, carrying three cans of Pepsi.

They sat together and began to eat.

4

After her shower, Penny felt much better. Her skin felt alive and light, almost tingling. She put on her silk pajamas—shorts and a tank top. The shiny fabric clung to her damp skin. She grabbed her robe from the hook on the back of the door. She put it on, tying the belt taut in front. It felt glued to her arms, but she wasn't going to take it off until bedtime. She would never hear the end of it from the girls about how skimpy her pajamas were.

Penny opened the door. The steam from the water swirled out into the hall. The air out here felt much cooler since they'd turned on the a/c.

She was about to head for the stairs when movement to her left caught her attention. Spinning around, she involuntarily brought up her hands.

And made Ashley jump back with a gasp. "Jeez!"

Penny dropped her hands. "Ash! Don't sneak up on me like that!"

"Sneak up? I was going to take a shower!" She held up the clothes and towel bundled in her hand. "Is that not allowed now?"

Penny took a deep breath. "Of course it is. Sorry. I guess I'm still a little jumpy from earlier."

Ashley nodded. Then a smile started to form on her face. "Maybe you should give Mr. Lawman a call. I bet he'd like to settle those nerves."

Penny's mouth dropped open. "Ash! Watch your mouth!" She started laughing.

"I'm just saying. I saw how he was looking at you."

Penny shook her head. "No thanks. I had the chance many times. Not my type."

"Too bad," said Ashley, heading toward the bathroom. "Maybe one day you'll find a guy worthy of your time." She entered the bathroom and closed the door.

Penny stared at the closed door for several seconds. A lot of thoughts flickered through her mind. She could have told Ashley there was only one man she'd loved and there would only be one man—her father. She doubted Ashley would understand that. Her eldest daughter just didn't like the idea of her mother spending so much time alone.

I'm not alone. I have Anna.

And she'd said that to Ashley many times whenever the subject was brought up.

Ashley's response was always the same: "But Anna will be going to college at some point, too."

Penny's throat tightened. She swallowed the lump that had been forming.

Not right now. Don't start feeling down already.

Penny marched downstairs and went straight for the kitchen. Opening the fridge, she saw the wine bottle on the rack. Other than Pepsi cans, water bottles, and clear baggies of sandwich meat, it was alone in there.

Should I have wine now?

She'd set up her laptop on the dining table after they'd eaten, planning to work on the book tonight. The first draft was due in two months, and she had a lot more to write. It still felt unreal that a publisher had reached out to her and asked if she'd be interested in writing a biography about her movie career. Mike, the editor, was a fan of her film work and wanted her to cover everything from how she was first brought into martial arts films, her training, and how all of it structured the life she led.

It had been therapeutic at times, sad at others. Overall, she'd discovered she had a love for writing that she didn't know she had. Always a heavy reader most of her life, she'd never attempted to write anything until this book.

And she loved doing it. Maybe she'd write something fictional when the biography was all done. She'd pitched many martial arts movies over the years. A lot of them became feature films, but others never made it to the script stage. She kept the treatments based on her ideas in a special file folder on a hard drive back in Georgia. Maybe she could flesh some of them out into novels.

Pitch the idea to Mike. See if he likes it.

She figured he would love it. But would anybody read a book that was written like a martial arts flick that came out in the early 90s?

"Let's drink," she muttered. She pulled out the bottle. Since she'd forgotten to bring any wine glasses, she grabbed a red plastic cup from the bag they'd bought at the store while on the road. Then she headed for the dining room. As she walked by the doors that led to the back porch, she saw one was slightly open, a bar of open space between the door and frame. The curtain fluttered inward from a weak breeze outside.

Penny let the bottle slide down her hand, gripping it high up on the neck. She turned it over, holding it with the fat end up. The cup was still in her other hand. She caught a glimpse of herself in the reflection of the dim light of the dining area on the glass door. It would have been funny if she weren't so concerned about why the door was open. She looked like a cave dweller, hair wet and wavy around her face and shoulders. Clutching the bottle as if it were a club she was about to bash somebody with.

She tried to put the incident at the gas station out of her mind by telling herself they wouldn't try it again. And even if they wanted to, how would they know where to find them?

Small town. Everybody knows everything.

They couldn't have figured it out already. They would, though, she knew.

So what?

Penny moved across the floor, stepping on the balls of her feet and rolling them forward to silence her approach. She heard something scuttle outside, a light brushing of feet on the wooden deck. She reached for the door.

It whirred open in front of her.

Stepping back, Penny turned and prepared herself to swing.

Anna stepped inside, glanced at Penny, and let out a shriek. She jumped backward through the doorway and was swallowed by the night.

Gasping, Penny hurried over to the door. "Anna!"

She could see her daughter standing under the porch light, a hand to her chest. Her legs were bare under the baggy hoody she had on. The odor of cigarettes hung in the air.

Penny tilted her head. "Smoking? Really?"

"I thought you went to bed!"

Penny held up the wine bottle. "Not yet. You're smoking?"

"A little."

"How long has this been going on?"

"I don't know. Not long."

"A month? Two?"

"A little over a year, I guess."

Penny was sure the shock showed on her face. Anna's head sagged as she grimaced.

"You're not even eighteen yet. How are you even getting them if you can't legally until you're twenty-one?"

"I have people do that for me." She reached into the hoody she had on and retrieved the pack. She fished one out.

Is she really about to smoke in front of me?

It looked like that was exactly what she was about to do. She snatched the cigarette from Anna's hand. It wasn't until her daughter went for her lighter that she noticed it was no longer pinched between her thumb and forefinger. Her head swiveled toward Penny. "Are you serious?"

Penny snapped the cigarette in half. "Very."

"Maybe you should smoke one, Mom. You're wound up tight tonight."

"I have this, thank you." She held up the wine bottle again. Liquid sloshed inside.

Anna frowned. Her face looked pale in the dim light. Moths fluttered around her. "You worried about those guys from earlier?"

"I wasn't until I saw the door open."

Anna made a coughing sound as she shook her head. Penny studied her. She noted her posture, the slouched shoulders, and how her arms were bent and kept close to her chest. She held the cigarettes in one hand, the lighter in the other.

"Are *you* worried about them?" Penny asked.

"Me?" She made a *pffft* sound with her lips. "Sure."

"You are, aren't you?"

Anna dropped the good-humored act. She shrugged. "I don't know. I didn't think we'd have to worry about that stuff while we were here."

"That's the problem," said Penny. She peeled the foil away from the top of the bottle. "We have to worry about that everywhere."

"You think you can teach me?"

Penny looked at her daughter. She suddenly looked like a little girl again, staring back at her with nervous eyes. "Teach you?"

"Yeah. Teach me to do what you do. The…" She held up her hand in a fist and made a swiping motion through the air. "You slap at that stuff."

"Slap?"

"You're good at it."

"Well, just say I'm good at it."

"I did."

Smiling, Penny set the cup on the deck rail. She opened the bottle, tilted it to her mouth, and drank.

"So much for taking it easy," said Anna, referencing the ignored cup.

The wine tasted cool and good. When she lowered it, she nodded. "If you really want to learn, I can teach you."

"Yes!" She pumped her fists.

"Listen. Before you get all excited, you need to understand that this won't be easy. You'll have to do *a lot* of physical work."

"I can do that."

"I've barely seen you lift anything more than your phone."

"Ouch, Mom."

"It's true. You will have to train. A lot. And smoking isn't going to help you at all."

"That's fine with me. See, I'm already good at some stuff. Watch this!" Anna stepped back, shifted onto her left foot, and kicked out with the right. It looked comically awful, but the way Anna was so proud of herself, Penny realized it had been a serious demonstration of her abilities. "What do you think?"

Penny took another heavy swig. In a breathy voice, she said, "Wow."

"I know." Anna rolled her eyebrows, a trait she'd picked up from her father.

Right then, she looked a lot like him, the eyes and nose. Penny's throat tightened.

"What now, Mom? You keep getting all emo and sh-stuff."

"Emo?"

"Yeah." She put a fingertip under her eye and ran it down her cheek.

"Is that supposed to be tears?"

"Yeah."

Penny shook her head. "Go to bed, huh? I've got some writing to do."

"I won't be able to sleep for a while. I'll probably just goof off on my phone, watch videos."

"Fine."

"Love you, Mom."

"Love you, too, honey."

Anna was about to walk back inside the cabin. Penny held out her hand.

"What?" Anna asked.

"The cigarettes."

"Aw, Mom."

"You said you want to train. No cigarettes."

"Can I just finish this pack first?"

"Are you seriously asking your mother if you can keep smoking underage?"

"How much trouble would I be in if I was?"

"A lot."

"Here you go." She held out the pack and the lighter.

Penny took them, dropping them in the pocket of her robe. "Goodnight."

"Goodnight." Anna went back inside.

Penny drank from the wine bottle for a few minutes, staring out at the darkened woods. The trees lightly swayed, the leaves rattling in the breeze. The plastic cup was blown off the railing. It clattered down the side of the cabin and went quiet when it hit the grass.

Was a storm coming? She looked up. The sky was clear. The half-moon was bright, throwing washed-out light over everything.

No storm.

Just one of those summer night breezes that felt so wonderful. Penny took a deep breath, inhaling the sweet aroma of the woods. The sounds and smells combined into a pleasant atmosphere that she hadn't realized how much she'd missed.

She was raising the bottle to her lips again when she saw a streak of light far off in the woods. It swiped through the trees, then vanished. Blinking, Penny focused on the spot for several minutes. It never repeated.

Had it been there at all?

Looked like a flashlight.

Penny watched the woods, holding her breath.

The light never appeared again.

Sighing, Penny walked back inside. She'd look for the red cup in the morning.

Locking the door behind her, she headed for the dining room. She had some writing to do.

5

It took Penny a little longer to find her groove than normal. Maybe it was from being in the cabin, with all its unfamiliar, yet also very familiar, sounds and smells. Or maybe it was being able to hear the girls moving around upstairs. She'd been able to hear the water in the pipes behind the walls while Ashley was showering. When the rushing sounds went quiet, Penny knew her oldest daughter was done.

Now, it was mostly quiet, save for the consistent trilling of crickets and frogs outside. That was a noise she relished, though. She hoped they never stopped.

After rereading what she'd written yesterday, she went back to work on a chapter about Alex training her. She'd already shared the story about how she'd moved to California with hopes of working in soap operas or sitcoms. Because of her height, and what she considered to be boring plain looks, she'd doubted she'd ever make it in movies unless it was a small supporting role.

She'd been in LA for three months when she met Alex Chambers. She was on the beach, rethinking her decisions after not getting another part for a TV show. Finding auditions hadn't been hard. Getting hired had been impossible. Here and there she'd get some day player work, earn a couple hundred bucks and a free meal, and was sent on her way.

More than once, a producer would ask her to stay behind after an audition that didn't go well. He'd give her a card for a buddy of his who was making a movie. She'd call the number with enthusiasm, only to learn it was a job to star in a porno. It had happened so often that she was beginning to think fucking strangers for cash was all she'd be good for in Hollywood.

Sitting on a towel that day, hugging her bare legs and staring at the crashing waves, she'd noticed the shadow wipe over her. Looking up, she saw a handsome man staring down at her. His black hair was shiny as it fluttered in the wind. Shirtless, his toned body was lightly tanned and slick under a sheen of suntan oil.

"Searching for somebody?" he asked.

"Excuse me?"

"The way you're staring at those waves, I thought you'd lost something out there."

A corner of Penny's mouth tilted upward. He was *really* cute. She liked the dimples on his cheeks when he smiled. "Just my dignity."

"Oh." Alex turned and stared at the ocean. "Out there?"

Penny nodded. "I think a shark got it."

"That's terrible." Putting his hands on his hips, he peered at the whitecaps. "They didn't say there were any sharks at the beach today. Wait…There it is. I see your dignity." He started walking toward the water. He wore swimming trunks and nothing else. The muscles in his back undulated with each step. He was thin, but toned, and lined with muscle.

Confused, Penny watched the handsome man go into the water. The waves crashed against him, climbing him. He ducked under the water.

What the hell's he doing?

She gazed at the ocean, watching the frothy water crash and thin out. He never resurfaced.

A few minutes later, she wondered if he was ever going to. "What the hell?" she muttered, leaning forward. She stretched out her legs. "Did he drown?"

The current didn't look very strong, but maybe he'd been pulled out deeper by it. She saw his lean body, curling and folding as he was sucked further into darker waters.

"Here's your dignity."

Penny jumped at Alex's voice. He was standing beside her again, dripping. In the flat of his hand was a sand dollar.

"How'd you do that?" she asked, laughing.

"Do what?"

"I was watching the water. I…you…never came out."

"Yes, I did. Here I am." He held out his arms. His abdominal muscles flexed.

Smirking, Penny shook her head. "Nice trick." She snatched the sand dollar from his hand. "How many girls you impress with that move?"

"Are you impressed?"

"Very."

"Then, one girl."

"Oh…" Penny felt heat in her cheeks that wasn't caused by the sun. "Smooth," she muttered and looked at the sand dollar.

"May I sit?" He motioned toward the beach blanket she was perched on.

"Well, you did find this for me, so I guess."

Alex sat down and introduced himself. Holding out his hand, he asked her name. Shaking his hand, she told him.

He made it easy to talk to. Probably because he did a lot of the talking at first. And he was funny. He made her laugh a lot while they sat on the blanket.

"That accent doesn't sound local," he said.

Penny snorted. "There's not a hick area in California?"

"Not the kind you'd want to claim."

"I see."

"Where are you from?"

"North Carolina."

"Wow! That's the other side of the country!"

"Believe me. I know. I took a bus out here."

"Jesus. Today?"

Penny couldn't tell if he was being serious or not. "No. A couple months ago."

"Let me guess. Came here to be in the movies."

"Wrong."

"You're kidding. You look like that, and you *don't* want to be in the movies?"

Penny's skin flushed. "Oh, stop. I don't look like anything."

"Look around you. You're the prettiest one out here."

"Trying to pick me up?"

"Is it working?"

Penny felt like fire was blazing under her skin. "No comment."

"So, no movies. Why LA?"

"Not movies, no. Sitcoms, yes. Maybe the soaps. Figured I could play a bookworm daughter or the girlfriend or something."

"Way too pretty for that. I look at you, and I see a superhero."

"Oh, stop. You can quit blowing smoke. You're already doing a good job and breaking down my walls."

"I'm being serious. Have you ever done any gymnastics or cheerleading?"

Penny tilted her head. She'd taken gymnastics for years and had been really good at it. But she'd outgrown the love for it when she was a teenager. She'd tried out for the cheerleading squad every year, but never made the cut. She figured it was because she just wasn't popular enough to be among the other girls.

"Maybe," she said. "Why are you asking? If you suggest I should go be in an adult film, I'll bury you in the sand headfirst."

Alex laughed. "No. No way. I'm taking that response as a 'yes' on the gymnastics thing. Good." His eyes roamed her. "You're in great shape, too. I think you'd be perfect."

Penny kind of liked how he was looking at her, how his eyes seemed to pull her into their brown deepness. But she didn't enjoy how ominous he was being. Why didn't he just come out and say what he clearly wanted to say?

She asked him.

"Want to get right to it, huh?" he asked.

"Better than the long way you're taking to get to your point."

Smiling, he nodded. "Point taken. I didn't want you to blow me off right away. Thought I'd give you some of my charm first."

"Is that what all that was?"

"Wasn't it charming?"

Penny smirked.

Alex laughed. It was a nice laugh that made his whole face light up. "I saw you earlier and thought, 'What the hell? What's the worst that could happen?'" He took a deep breath.

Penny smiled. The guy seemed so self-confident just minutes before. Now that it was time for him to make his move, he was getting bashful.

"Here it goes," he said. He looked her in the eye. "Have you ever taken any martial arts?"

And that question was what led to her joining Alex's stunt crew on a film being shot in Thailand called *Lady Striker*. It was a low budget action movie starring Vanessa Crowe as Brenda Brown, an American crime-fighting reporter, fluent in martial arts. Ms. Brown always seemed to get caught up in some sort of violent trouble while investigating a murder, a costly theft, a gang of robbers, or an ancient Chinese curse that was accidentally unleashed upon the world.

Penny started off as a background stunt performer. She knew how to fall, so Alex would always put her in the best combat spots. The directors and producers really enjoyed working with Alex, and they began to take notice of Penny's improvement in each production. It was Alex's training that helped her. He'd been a student of various martial arts teachers. He'd even created a style of his own that borrowed from several others that he'd altered or improved.

Penny was a quick learner. The passion to be taught flowed through her. Alex even said, more than once, it was as if she'd been created to learn the arts. Created to perform. And created to fight.

She hadn't agreed with him, but his words always seemed to make her feel like she could do anything. Plus, martial arts filled a void inside her that had been there as far back as she could remember. It didn't make her complete, though. Alex was the final piece that did that. Their love had been instant, but Penny fought it for months before she could no longer. She'd worried that becoming involved with her trainer and boss would only lead to disaster.

She'd been right, but the disaster hadn't come from their embracing their love. The producers of the *Lady Striker* series were growing tired of Vanessa Crowe's antics and movie star attitude. They'd grown to appreciate and value Penny's hard work and dedication. Plus, she was overly respectable to their culture and lifestyles.

Penny was cast as Machete Monroe, the villain of the final *Lady Striker* movie. The final fight ended with Brenda Brown's demise. The next film in the series was a rebranding called *Machete Mama,* and all about the character's evolution from the villain to the hero. She was a flawed character, complicated, and riddled with guilt from killing Brenda Brown.

At one time, she'd been her killer. Now, she'd be her avenger.

Penny leaned back in the chair, stretching. She read over Machete Mama's vow, which became the logline for the first two movies. She smiled. Alex had come up with it himself. The writers loved it.

Penny scrolled back through the pages in her Word file, looking over what all she'd done tonight.

Wow. Eight pages.

She hadn't even noticed how long she'd been pecking away at the keys without stopping. She was sweating under her top. More trickled down from her hairline. Going back in time in her mind had been stressful yet also relieving.

The chair was making her back hurt, so she stood up and stretched. She lifted her foot, gripped her heel, and pulled her leg up and straight. She leaned her head against the top of her foot and sighed at the tingly pulling she felt all through her. She repeated the stretch with the other leg, then folded herself backward, putting both feet flat on the floor. She reached behind her, groaning as she gripped her ankles in a shape like a human table.

Alex's favorite position.

The memory of him coming into their exercise room and finding her on the mat, performing this pose materialized in her mind. They'd made love with Penny bent backward, her thighs parted while Alex stood between her, thrusting. His hands roamed her, squeezed her breasts, and pinched her nipples. Six weeks later, her doctor informed her that she was pregnant with Ashley.

Penny stood up straight. It was a good memory, but it often left her feeling hollow and alone. She stepped back over to the chair. She looked at her laptop.

She'd flown through the training bits, maybe a little too quickly. During her rewrite, she might thicken it up some, add more details about the practices and arts that Alex taught her. She knew why she'd been taking shortcuts in this first draft, skimping certain aspects of what led to her becoming one of the biggest stars in Hong Kong Action Cinema.

Vanessa Crowe.

Their real-life feud was legendary in the world of action entertainment. Losing her job as Lady Striker, Vanessa sank into a downward spiral of anger and drugs. Tantrums on other movie sets eventually got her blacklisted. The studios that would still work with her usually regretted it. She went from being the most loved to the most reviled in all martial arts cinema. And Penny rose to the top, taking her spot without even trying to or really wanting it.

Vanessa blamed Penny for her downfall. Angry letters started being delivered, then packages of headless birds. Though they weren't signed, nor was there a return address, Penny knew who'd sent them.

The phone calls started soon after that. Then came the black car that followed her everywhere, even to the girls' daycare and school, and eventually their family outings. One time, Alex saw the car parked near theirs at the movie theater. He marched over to confront the driver, but the car sped away before he got close enough.

Again, Penny knew it was Vanessa. Alex believed her. Too bad nobody else had.

The police hadn't been able to help. So, the harassment continued, getting worse—sicker and meaner. A lunatic's obsession that was all focused on Penny.

They moved to Georgia, hoping to flee it all. Not just harassment, but also life in Hollywood. The cost of living in the tiny country town of Whereville was much lower than LA. They were able to afford a large house deep in the woods for less than what they had been paying for a small house in the Hollywood Hills.

The area was gorgeous. Peaceful. Penny told Alex how she felt like a Disney Princess most mornings during her walks from all the wildlife that she would see.

For a long time, everything was better.

Then it wasn't.

Vanessa found them.

Penny, standing at the dining table, stared at the blinking cursor on the laptop screen for several more seconds. Shaking her head, she closed the laptop, killing the dim light in the room. She hadn't decided yet how deep she was going to go into the Vanessa Crowe material.

I can't tell them everything.

The book would become a killer's confession if she revealed the complete truth.

Penny realized she was shaking. She took a deep breath, closed her eyes, and held the air in her lungs. As she slowly let it out, she visualized clouds floating past her as if she were soaring through the fluffy white. The sky behind them was a rich blue, bright and warm, with a golden mist bordering the visual. She saw Alex's face, his smile. Then she could feel his arms around her, holding her.

Then she saw him on the ground, his stomach sliced open while Penny crouched beside him, holding the flaps of flesh together to keep his guts inside.

Penny jerked rigid. Her eyes snapped open. She looked around. She was back in the dining room. The darkness felt heavy, pressing down on her. If she didn't get out of this room, she would be crushed under its murky weight.

Snatching the wine bottle from the table, she rushed into the kitchen. The lights under the cupboards were on, spreading a comfortable luminosity around the room. It turned the window above the sink into an obsidian mirror. She saw the faint smudge of herself in the reflection, standing with the wine bottle held out like a lantern. Her robe looked like an ancient gown.

Tilting the bottle up to her lips, she took a few gulps. The wine wasn't as chilled as it had been, but she couldn't care less. It still rinsed a calming flow down her throat. Breathless, she set the bottle on the counter. That was better. Chugging the bottle until it was empty would help even more, would make her numb.

Make me forget.

At least for tonight. Until the memory of Alex dying in her arms came back tomorrow. The months after he was taken from her and the girls, Penny drowned the memories with alcohol. It helped with erasing the images, but ruined so much else. She got control of herself before she fractured her relationship with her daughters. They had needed her to be strong for them, to teach them strength, just as Alex had taught her.

But they'd been so young then.

They hardly remembered their father now.

They knew him, though, through Penny. She kept him alive for them with stories, photographs, and, of course, their film library.

Penny grabbed the wine bottle and carried it over to the sink. Turning it upside down, she poured out the rest. Its glugging sounds were loud in the quiet kitchen. When the bottle was empty, she held it by the neck.

It's quiet up there.

She looked at the ceiling. She didn't hear Ashley or Anna moving around anymore. It was pretty late, so they were most likely asleep.

That's where you need to be, kiddo.

It'd been a long day of driving and stress. The incident at the gas station had only added to her exhaustion.

She was ready to sleep.

The first thing she needed to do was get rid of the empty bottle, then check to make sure all the doors were locked. The alarm system hadn't been activated yet, which she didn't like. But she'd have to deal with it until somebody from the alarm place came out to set it up.

A lamp was on in the living room. Soft light spilled out into the hallway between the stairs. All the curtains were closed, blocking out the night. Penny hated having curtains open when it wasn't daylight outside. People could see you, but you couldn't see them even if they were standing right outside.

Penny reached the front door. She could tell it was locked, but she would have to unlock it to toss the bottle outside with the trash. She wanted it out of her sight. She was proud of herself for not drinking all the wine at once, but knew the girls would probably think she did. Especially when they saw it with the trash outside.

She pinched the lock. The clack of the deadbolt twisting back resounded around her. Flinching, she looked back at the stairs, expecting to hear the girls yelling about the noise. They didn't.

Penny opened the door.

And jumped back as the man rushed at her.

1

In her quick glimpse of the man, she saw that he was wearing a black ski mask and dark clothes.

And the baseball bat he was holding was swinging at her face.

Bending sideways, she dodged the bat. She spun around, swinging the wine bottle. It connected with the back of his head with a hollow clang. Unlike in the movies, it didn't explode into a million shards. Instead, it remained intact, sending a jolt up her arm and the intruder sprawling on the floor.

Penny jumped over his limp form, then looked outside. She didn't see anyone else out there. Stepping back, she bent over. She'd need both hands for this. She put down the bottle, grabbed his pants' leg, and dragged him outside. His head bounced over the threshold. He started to moan.

Penny brought her bare foot down on his masked face, silencing him. She checked one more time for another one, then got back inside and shut the door. The bat was still on the floor. After locking the door, she snatched it. She stood at the bottom of the stairs, looking up into the dark.

"Ash! Anna! Get up!" She waited for a second. "Girls!"

"H-huh…?" came the groggy reply of her oldest daughter.

"Get up! Somebody tried to break in!"

"What!"

She needed her phone, needed to call 911. She felt her pockets and sighed with relief when she felt the bulge in the left one. Reaching in, she tugged out Anna's pack of cigarettes.

"Shit!" she gasped.

Something whammed the door hard enough to rattle the thick wood in the frame. Penny spun around, bringing up the bat as two more blows sent tremors through the floor. She heard wood starting to crack.

Where the hell's my phone?

She didn't want to leave her spot and take her eyes off the door, but she needed to find her phone. She ran into the dining room. On the table was her laptop. The phone wasn't there.

Damn it!

"Ashley!" she yelled. "Call nine-one-one!"

Ashley's screams echoed through the ceiling.

No!

Penny dashed back to the stairs, ignoring the pounding on the door. Just as she started to climb, she heard wood break behind her. Looking over her shoulder, she saw the edge of an ax poking through, twisting, then vanish as it was pulled back out. Another loud hit and the ax tip appeared again.

Ashley took the stairs three at a time, stretching her legs as far as they would go. She made it to the top in two seconds.

As she ran up the short hall, she slapped the light switch on her way. Weak light dropped down from the old lightbulb in the dusty glass cover. Anna stepped out from the room to the right, her face pale and eyes bulging.

"Stay in there," Penny said. "Lock your door and call the—"

She saw the man behind her, pressed against Anna's back. He held a knife to the side of Anna's neck. Like the guy downstairs, he also wore a black ski mask. His grinning mouth showed in the bottom hole. The lips were ringed with beard stubble.

Penny threw the bat. It spun through the air, coming close enough to Anna to ruffle her hair. Missing her head, it made a *bonk* when it hit the man's exposed left eye. He let out a grunt and flew back into the room. Anna, realizing what had just happened, stumbled forward. She was trembling all over and starting to cry.

Penny took Anna's hand as she ran by, pulling her away from the room. It was like dragging a heavy mannequin. Her youngest daughter's legs didn't seem like they wanted to work.

"Do you have your phone?" she asked.

Anna blinked. "Huh?"

"Your phone! Do you have it?"

"It's…" She looked over her shoulder. "In my…" She screamed when the man staggered out of the room, bent over. He held a hand over his eye.

Penny spun around, kicking him in the throat. Making strangled sounds, he lurched back into the darkness again. Penny slammed the door hard enough to crack the paneling.

She pulled the door one more time, wedging it in the frame. It should keep the guy away for a while. But it also locked Anna's phone in there.

It didn't matter. Getting to Ashley now was more important.

As if to agree, Ashley screamed from the room across the hall. Penny yanked Anna out of the way, then ran at the door, jumping. She lowered her shoulder. It rammed the door, throwing it open. Penny ran into the room.

She saw Ashley on the bed. On her back and naked from the waist down, her oldest daughter's spread legs were kicking at the mattress as the guy crouched between them pushed his pants down his bare ass with one hand. The other hand clutched Ashely's wrists on the bed above her head. Her long T-shirt had been ripped open, exposing her breasts.

The masked man spotted Penny and gasped.

Penny absorbed the images before her, letting the rage they caused become fuel for her actions. Her mind shut off, and all she saw was red, like watching a 3D movie with broken glasses.

Her fist connected with his jaw, knocking his head sideways. His erection bounced as he fell. He hit the floor, rolling backwards. His ass squeaked on the hardwood.

Penny snatched Ashley's hand, jerked her to her feet, and spun her around. The ripped T-shirt fell down her, getting hung on her hips. Her breasts shook as she sobbed.

Pulling off her own robe, Penny wrapped it around Ashley's shoulders. "Get over there with your sister!" She shoved Ashley into Anna.

Penny felt better without the robe, lighter in only her shorts and tank top. Her skin was glossy with sweat, making the diaphanous pajamas cling to her.

"Fuckin' hot, Mama," said the guy on the floor. He started to laugh. "You sleep in that?"

Levi.

"I should've known," said Penny.

"You really should've." He got to his knees, pulling off the ski mask. His hair was mussed and sweaty. His face was red. "Guess I don't need this anymore." Standing up, he tucked his hard cock back in his pants, buttoning them. "I've been thinking about this ever since the gas station."

"So have I."

"Thinking about me? Awww. That's sweet." He grabbed the large hunting knife from the bed. Penny hadn't noticed it before. It was probably what he used to slash Ashley's shirt. He looked at her breasts again, whistling. "I'm going to suck on them. One way or another."

"Come get 'em."

"Gladly."

Levi ran at her, raising the knife. Penny kicked him in the crotch. She felt the hard bulge of his penis snap under her heel.

Levi's hollering turned into a squeak. Eyes crossing, he dropped to his knees. The knife fell from his hands. Catching it, Penny plunged the blade into Levi's throat.

Behind her, Ashley and Anna screamed. She looked over and saw they were reacting to their mother's violent act. Their expressions were something they might have given to a feral animal ripping apart a kitten. "Don't look," she said.

Ashley turned her head, forcing Anna to look away as well.

Penny looked back at Levi. His wide eyes were gazing at her, filled with hurt and shock. She leaned down close to his face. Blood trickled from the corners of his mouth, dribbling off his chin.

"You should have stayed away from my family."

An image of Vanessa Crowe flashed in her mind—on her knees, bloody and battered, her clothes torn as she swayed near the edge of the ravine. The rushing water of the mountains was fifty feet below them. The machete was held against the defeated woman's smooth throat.

"Do it!" Vanessa growled through her heavy breaths.

Levi coughed. Blood shot out of his mouth, sprinkling Penny's face with warm dots and snapping her back to the present. Gripping the hilt, Penny yanked sideways. The blade ripped his throat open, dumping blood with sounds like air leaking from a tire.

Her daughters whimpered. Though they'd obeyed and kept their eyes away, it did nothing to protect them from the sounds of her killing somebody.

Penny stepped back, letting Levi drop to the floor. She stepped away from the spreading puddle of blood. Turning to her daughters, she said, "Where's your phone, Ash?"

Ashley, lips quivering, said, "He-he-he smashed it."

"Forget it. Let's get to the car and get out of her."

"Can I get dressed?" said Ashley.

"No time. Come on!"

Penny led them back to the stairs. They were halfway down when the front door broke open. The man outside charged in, shouting, holding an ax with two blades.

The girls screamed, drawing his attention to the stairs. That was fine, because Penny was already preparing for the confrontation. The intruder had climbed onto the first stair when Penny jumped, giving him two rapid kicks to his chest. As she came down, she swung out with the knife. He saw it coming and jumped back, dodging the swiping blade, and screamed in terror.

"Damn!" he yelled. His eyes inside the mask's holes showed fear. He blindly swung the ax as he spun around.

Penny stepped sideways, easily avoiding it, but didn't get the knife out of the way in time. It was knocked out of her hand with the clamor of colliding metal.

The ax blade chopped into Anna's arm.

Shrieking, Anna fell on Ashley, knocking her older sister against the wall. The intruder held the ax up. His eyes widened when he saw the blood slipping down the curved blade.

"Oh…shit…" he said.

Penny ran at him. He saw her coming and a shrill cry tore out of his mouth.

A moment later, Penny threw him through the remaining wedges of the door that were still attached by the hinges. Landing on his side, he bounced across the porch. The railing stopped him. He stayed there, unmoving, beside his buddy who'd been left there by Penny at the start of this assault.

One dead. Three down.

Penny stepped through the broken door, scanning the yard. She doubted there were any more. There had been four men at the gas station, and she'd taken out four men here.

She turned around. "Wait here. I need to get my keys."

"Don't leave us," said Anna, jaw trembling. She held her hand on her wound. Blood streamed from under her fingers.

"It'll just be a minute, baby. Are you okay?"

Anna nodded. "Just hurts."

"I know it does. I'll get you to the hospital. We can call the police from there."

It didn't take long for Penny to find her keys. She gave one last look for her phone, then rushed back to the front where her daughters were waiting.

Ashley was watching her. Her face was glossy under a mask of tears. "Can we go now?"

Nodding, Penny reached them. "Let me take her."

Ashley helped Anna lean against her, then braced her uninjured arm behind Penny's neck.

"Got her?" asked Ashley.

"Yeah."

Anna moaned a response.

Ashley walked away from them.

"Where are you going?" asked Penny.

"Our shoes." Their shoes were on the mat beside the door. Ashley slid her feet into hers first, then picked up Penny's and Ashley's pairs. A set in each hand, she hurried back to them and placed them at their feet. "I'll help Anna."

Penny stuffed her bare feet into her shoes just as Ashley finished assisting Anna with hers. "Let's get the hell out of here."

The girls gasped when they saw the men on the porch. Though they were both down, just the sight of them must've been terrifying. Penny remembered what Levi was about to do to Ashley. She saw his bare ass in her mind, wedged between Ashley's spread legs. Had he put it inside her? Did he violate her?

The hospital would do a test.

I killed him.

And she felt no guilt about it.

"Mom!" Ashley went ahead of them, pointing at the car. "Look!"

At first, Penny didn't know what she was pointing at. Then she saw where her finger was aimed.

The tires…

All four had been slashed.

Penny felt a pang of worry and quickly shoved it aside. "We'll walk."

"It's so far," said Anna.

"Would you rather stay here?" said Ashley, her voice cracking.

"No!"

"Girls!" Penny saw how they flinched and felt bad. "Sorry. I didn't mean to yell. But walking is our only option right now. We'll flag somebody down."

"But the way we're dressed," said Ashley. "What if…?"

Ashley was naked under Penny's robe. Anna had on a sleep shirt that reached her knees. It was easy to tell she wasn't wearing a bra. She didn't know if she had panties on.

Penny wasn't wearing any underwear at all beneath her silky tank top and shorts. But she also wasn't worried about any scumbags finding them. "I'll handle it."

"Yeah," said Anna, nodding. "You will."

Before they started walking, Penny got the first-aid kit from the car. There wasn't much inside it, but she managed to somewhat dress Anna's gash with some bandages.

"Let me help you," said Penny.

Anna shook her head. "I'm okay. It'll just slow us down. I'll walk."

"Are you sure?"

"Yes. I just wanna get out of here."

"Same here," said Ashley.

"Then let's go."

They were almost to the end of the driveway and still hadn't come across their attackers' vehicle. Penny assumed they'd stashed it somewhere on the road and hiked back to the cabin. It didn't really matter how they got there. They'd invaded the cabin with intentions to harm them all.

To rape us.

Another image of Ashley underneath Levi flickered in her mind.

He better not have gotten...

Penny stopped herself from thinking about it. Now wasn't the time. Getting help was what she needed to focus on. Keeping the girls safe.

She kept expecting the men to come after them. At times, she almost hoped they would. That way, she could kill them all, like Levi. She should've done that to begin with. But remembering how Ashley and Anna had looked at her after she'd jammed the knife in the young man's throat made her feel awful. Maybe she shouldn't have killed him, either.

They'll never forget it.

Sure, she'd saved them, but she'd also added to their trauma. They'd probably have nightmares about it for years, maybe forever.

And I still have his blood on me.

She could feel it on her face, sticky dots that crackled when they stretched.

"Are you okay?" asked Ashley.

Penny thought she was talking to Anna, who'd managed to keep walking, albeit at a lethargic pace. Then she noticed Ashley, beside her, was looking at her. "Me?"

"Yeah. You look lost in your head." Ashley's dark hair hung down, hiding most of her face except for the pale knobs of her cheekbones. Her eyes seemed to shimmer in the moonlight.

"I'm not okay," she admitted. "But we'll be fine."

They reached the road a few minutes later. It was dark in either direction except for spots here and there that were mottled with moonlight. To the left led deeper into the mountain, curving into the trees not far past her driveway. Going right would lead them into town, though it would be hours before they got there.

Unless somebody came along and helped.

"Do either of you need to rest?" Penny asked. They told her they didn't. "Then let's go."

They walked in the right lane, their footfalls quiet on the blacktop. The road was a pale line between strips of wilderness on either side. Moonlight cast everything in a silver glaze.

"I never thought I'd hate the quiet," said Ashley. "It's *too* quiet."

Penny had to agree. Even the nightlife seemed to be on pause.

Which made hearing the hum of the engine even easier.

"What's that?" said Anna. "Do you hear that?"

"What?" said Ashley.

"I do," said Penny.

"Is that a car?" asked Anna.

Penny heard the shift in tone as gears changed. "I think it is. It's coming from behind us."

"Shit," said Ashley. "It's them!"

A squeaky sound came from Anna's throat.

"I don't think so," said Penny.

"You don't?"

"Unless they're driving something other than that truck. Remember, they left in that truck earlier. The engine is too quiet."

"It's getting closer," said Ashley.

Penny could see shaky light on the road reaching out from the side of the trees. Whoever was coming was about to take that curve. Soon as they did, the headlights would be pointed straight at them.

She didn't feel quite so confident anymore. It very well could be the other three. They'd found Levi's dead body and were coming after them. "Get off the road."

"Why?" said Ashley.

"Now."

The three of them stepped off the asphalt and into the overgrown grass on the roadside. The fuzzy tips of the weeds tickled Penny's shins. Headlights appeared at the curve, aimed at them. The engine noise rose as the car accelerated.

It dropped away with the squealing of tires.

They see us...

Penny took a deep breath, readying herself to fight again.

Lights appeared above the dark space over the headlights. Blue and white, they began to twirl, throwing rotating colors against the trees.

"It's a cop!" said Anna. "Thank God!"

Penny stepped out into the road. She kept her right hand at her side, ready to strike. "Stay there, girls."

"It's a cop, Mom," said Ashley.

"Just do what I say."

The driver's side door opened with a soft groan. The dark figure of the driver rose above the door. A flashlight clicked on. "Penny? That *is* you! What happened?"

"Charlie!" Penny said, nearly dropping to her knees as the tension flowed from her. "Thank God..."

"The guy from the gas station?" said Ashley.

Penny let out the deep breath she'd been holding. "Yes."

She saw Charlie step out from behind the open door. He wore his campaign hat. Taking it off, his cropped hair looked like bristles in the wriggling shadows. "Jesus H., Penny." He rushed over to them. "What happened?"

"Guys broke into the cabin," said Anna.

"Attacked us," said Ashley, talking over her sister.

Penny looked at Charlie. "It was the guys from earlier, from the gas station."

Charlie's eyes narrowed. "You're sure?"

She nodded. "Yes." She decided to leave out the part about killing Levi. Charlie would know soon enough.

"Jesus," he said. He shook his head. "All right. Let's you girls off the road." Noticing Anna, he winced. "You're bleeding. Are you okay?"

"She got hit with an ax," said Ashley.

"Damn." He held his arm out, motioning them to start moving. "Let's go. I'll get you to the hospital and call it in on the way."

"Thank you, Charlie," said Penny. "Thank you."

He looked at her. "I always get here too late with you. I guess you handled it."

"Not enough." She glanced at Anna, feeling a pull in her heart when she saw how pale she was. Saw how her eyes were darkening as they usually did whenever she was running a fever. "She's hurt."

"She'll be fine," said Charlie. He opened the back door of his SUV. A cage wall separated it from the front seat. "I know it doesn't look very friendly, but the seats are comfortable. Let me help you." He assisted Anna first, being careful around her arm. It helped to put Penny at ease even more, seeing him be so delicate with her daughter.

"Thank you," said Anna, once she was seated.

"No sweat, darlin'. Now we'll get your sister situated." He led Ashley around the back of the car. Penny started to follow but stopped when the rear passenger door opened. She saw Ashley climb in. "Watch your feet." Ashley looked down, then moved her legs. The robe had parted, showing her thighs. The door shut.

Penny could hear the crunches of Charlie's boots as he walked back around to where she was standing. "Now, let's take care of you."

Penny smiled. "I'm so glad you came along."

"Me too," he said.

Her smile died when she saw the taser in his hand was aimed at her. "What are you doing, Charlie?"

There was a springy sound, and three tabs launched out of the gun, spreading as they neared her. Penny knew there was no time to do anything about it. They stuck to her on three different sections of her torso, feeling like bee stings at first. When Charlie squeezed the trigger, hot pain zipped through her. She blinked and was suddenly on the ground, her body stiff and jerking as she sizzled under her skin.

The screams and cries of her girls were muffled through the glass. They banged on the windows, rattled the cage, but couldn't get out of the back seat.

Looking up, she saw Charlie standing over her. Three wires coiled upward to the tip of the oddly shaped gun in his hand. He lifted his finger. The pain shut off, releasing its paralyzing hold of her muscles. She felt drained, as if her arms and head were weighed down with anchors.

Charlie shook his head. "Can't let you get away, Penny. It's how it is."

"Guh…" Her throat throbbed as if hands had been slowly crushing it.

"Mom!" Ashley yelled. "Mom!"

Charlie shrugged.

Then his finger tightened around the trigger again.

D arkness.

Ethereal voices floated in the distance, far away at the end of a black tunnel. Penny understood she'd been unconscious. For how long, she didn't know.

Things felt different now. She was stretched out. She could feel her arms, but they were pulled taut above her. Her hands were stuck together, most likely bound. Her fingers were numb.

Her legs, spread wide, had tightness around her ankles. More bondage, she realized.

She'd been strapped down.

The darkness began to lift as she struggled to open her eyes. Light spilled in through the gap. It hurt like a fist punching into her eye sockets. In her blurry glance, she recognized she was in the master bedroom in the cabin. Her head was on a pillow, which meant she'd been tied down to the bed. She also saw the smeared shapes of people. The voices cleared for a moment, and she was able to make out:

"Ripped his throat open…" Then the words were floating again, drifting around her like fireflies. She tried to catch them, to hear them, but they were out of reach.

Empty blackness filled her again. She floated in the abyss, nothing around to hold onto, to keep her conscious.

Then a sharp, bitter smell filled her nostrils, suffocating her. The void around her pulled away as her eyes snapped open and she sucked in some air.

Charlie filled her vision, his shaved head tilted down at her. He pulled away the tiny tube of smelling salt. "There she is. You were out for a bit. Guess the taser made all that adrenaline crash, huh?"

Penny's throat was dry and scratchy. It hurt when she said, "Where are my girls?"

"They're entertaining my men." His mouth curled on the sides, showing his teeth. "And they're doing such a good job."

Penny twisted inside, hot anger surging through her. She shot up, slamming her head into Charlie's nose. There was a pop, then he groaned. She was secured to the bed, but her head was still free to fight.

Charlie fell onto his side on the mattress.

The young man from earlier, Tommy, hurried over to the bed. "Sheriff!"

Charlie quickly sat up, holding his nose with one hand. He held out the other to Tommy, stopping him. "It's okay, deputy. She didn't break it. She tried to, though."

"Deputy?" said Penny. She looked at Tommy. He stood there, looking smug. "You're a cop, too?"

"They're all my deputies," said Charlie. He wiggled his nose with his thumb and forefinger, moaning. His eyes were watery. "It's gonna swell, but it's not broken." Checking his fingers, he nodded. "Not even bleeding. Guess I need to be more careful, huh?"

He put his hand high up on her thigh and slid it even higher. Penny felt his fingers poking her folds. Twisting her hips, she moved away from him. She was naked, her silk pajamas gone.

Charlie's hand gripped a breast and squeezed. "My God," he said. "It feels even better than I imagined it would. You always had such nice tits. Back in high school, all the guys talked about them. You were the nerdy chick with a great rack and a hot ass. Drove us wild. And you knew it did. You were always okay with flauntin' it, showin' it off. But whenever I tried to touch? You stopped me. I even liked you, wanted to *date* you. But you…" He clucked his tongue. "I just wasn't good enough."

Penny tried to bring her arms down to block his dry, groping hand. The rope binding her wrists prevented them from moving. There was nothing she could do but let him have his fun.

What's happening to the girls?

There were two guys unaccounted for. She knew where the fourth was—dead in Ashley's bedroom.

"Why are you doing this, Charlie?"

"Levi, the one you killed? He's my deputy as well. *Was* my deputy. He's also my nephew. And he works for me."

Charlie's fingers found her nipple and pinched the tip. It hurt, but Penny held in her reaction. "What do you mean, works for you?"

"You're awfully chatty. Don't you want to know how your sweet daughters are entertaining my men?"

"You hurt either one of them, I'll kill you."

"Oh, I don't doubt that. That's why you're not getting untied." Charlie stood up. He wiggled his nose a few times, then nodded to himself, satisfied. He started unbuttoning his uniform shirt. "They're entertaining my men the same way you're about to entertain me."

Penny felt a cold bubble in her stomach. "That's what this is about? I wouldn't fuck you in high school?"

"No, no, no. Not completely. At first, it was just business. Doing what I was told. But Levi, remember all those things I said about him a minute ago? Well, I forgot to add that he's an idiot. Probably the biggest idiot I've ever met. Even more dumb than my sister. Remember Wynona?"

Penny did remember her. She was older than Penny by two years. She'd gotten in trouble at school for getting caught sucking the custodian's dick in a broom closet. She'd been expelled from school, and the custodian, whose name Penny couldn't remember, had gone to jail. She had no idea what happened to either of them.

Charlie held out his shirt. It hung from his hand. Tommy, who'd been standing by the doorway, stepped forward and took it. Folding it neatly, he put it on the empty dresser, then returned to his position by the doorway.

"Anyway," said Charlie. "Levi's an idiot because he got killed. He wasn't supposed to mess with the girls until the area was secure. He got overzealous. The dumbass. I'll have to figure out something to tell Wynona. Thanks for adding more shit to my day tomorrow."

"Am I supposed to cry about it?" she asked.

Charlie huffed through his nose. "You can step outside now, Tommy."

"Are you sure, sir?"

"You want to watch us or something, freak show?"

Tommy looked excited for a moment, then shook his head. "No, sir. I just didn't know if you wanted me to hang around to…make sure…"

"To make sure what?"

"That she doesn't fight back too hard."

Charlie laughed. "I want her to fight back as hard as she can. That's sort of the point. She can fight back and can't do nothin' about it!"

Nodding, Tommy stepped into the hallway.

"Tommy?"

"Yes, sir?"

"Close the door, please."

The door snicked shut.

Charlie stood beside the bed in a snug white T-shirt tucked into his uniform pants. It clung to his muscular arms. Back in school, he'd been a scrawny kid. But Penny could tell he worked out these days. From the size of his physique, it appeared he worked out a lot. "Alone at last."

Penny knew what was coming. She also knew Charlie had been right: there was nothing she could do to prevent it from happening. She took a deep breath and tried to find her peace. No matter what was happening to her in the physical world, her mind would be detached, never feeling any of it until her conscious thought returned.

She saw the clouds, saw the golden rays of light washing through. She could feel its embracing warmth pulling her closer.

Then all she saw was crimson saturating everything. Her insides began to burn. There was no peace to find right now.

All she felt was rage.

"If looks could kill," said Charlie. "Wow. I like it. Can't wait to see the look on your face when I shove my dick in your mouth."

She opened her mouth and clacked her teeth together a couple times.

Charlie smirked. "You would do that, wouldn't you?"

"Gobble it up."

Charlie stared at her for a long moment. "Hmmm. I'm still tempted." He unhooked his gun belt and let it drop. It thumped on the floor. Next, he unbuttoned his pants.

"Is this why you sent your boys here? So you could do this?"

"I told you—it was just business at first. But when you killed my idiot nephew, it became personal again."

"What kind of business?"

"Dirty business." He pushed his pants and underwear down in one motion. Bending over, he pulled his legs free and stood up. He held his pants out, the empty legs swaying beside him. "I'm not supposed to say anything. I've probably already said too much."

His hard on was a jutting pole between his legs. The head, massive and wide, capped the top of a shaft of veins. "Surprised?" he said. "Most people are."

Penny was very surprised. And repulsed. She felt tight and sick inside. That feeling wouldn't last long, though. Because Charlie was going to tear her apart.

He carried his pants over to the dresser where Tommy had put his shirt. He set the pants on top, then came back to the bed. In nothing but black socks, his cock bounced with each step he took. Sometimes it popped against his leg, making a dull smacking sound.

"There was a time, Penny, when I was pretty nuts about you. Now I just wanna nut in you." Laughing, he crawled up on the bed.

Penny grimaced. "You're sick."

"Maybe. If I am, it's only a little. I'm just doing my best in this shitty town. You had the right idea by getting out. If I could go back in time, I'd get out, too. But my dumbass took the exam and passed. Next thing I knew, I was training to be a deputy. Years later, and after a rigged election, I'm the sheriff. Have been for a while and don't plan on stopping anytime soon."

He shoved his knee between her clamped thighs, forcing them apart. Then he brought his other leg over, planting both knees on the mattress between her legs. Penny tried to close them, but his hips stopped her.

"The pay's good," he said, scooting closer. "And I have the side businesses. Keeps the money pouring in. I was put in charge of a lot of areas out here. I'm damn good at my job. And you're my bonus. I get to do what I want to you until the boss shows up tomorrow. That gives the rest of the night."

"The boss?" Penny frowned. "What the hell are you talking about?"

"You should've stayed away." He raised his fingers to his mouth, making sure Penny could see them. Then he stuck two in his mouth, sucking them in and out in a gross way.

Penny only watched. She could tell he wanted her to ask more questions about the things he was saying, that he wanted her to react to the disgusting sucking he was doing with his fingers. But she wouldn't give him the benefit of it. Sure, she was very curious about what he was talking about, and though she had a good idea what he was going to do next, she was tempted to try to talk him out of it.

Play dead, Penny.

She shut down, keeping her eyes locked on him.

He pulled his fingers from his mouth with a wet *pop*. Lowering his hand, the shiny fingers disappeared from

Penny's view. She felt them shove into her a moment later. She didn't even flinch. She wanted to, wanted to jerk back and scream at him. Instead, she breathed long and slow, focusing on her heartbeat, making sure it remained steady. It was a breathing exercise that Alex had taught her years ago for her anxiety. It kept her heart rate down and her mind flowing like a stream. He'd said, "Our minds get jumbled up like a beaver dam. All our worries and stresses start piling up. That makes our hearts beat too fast, which gets the blood pumping. Next thing we know, we're having a panic attack. Our worries need to stay moving, flowing through our mind until they're no longer a part of us."

Charlie frowned as he dug around. He didn't seem to like that she wasn't responding to his violating pokes. He pushed even harder, pulled out, and rammed his fingers inside hard enough to make her bounce. She held onto her breathing, focused on his dumb face.

Stared him in the eyes.

"Stop looking at me like that," he said. He rammed her again, shoving his hand against her soft ingress. His knuckles pushed inside.

That hurts. God. That fucking hurts!

Penny almost broke, but she found her rhythm again and breathed.

"You feel good in there," he said, pulling out his fingers. He stuck them in his mouth and suckled. When he was done, he pulled them out. "You taste good, too."

Penny's stomach lurched. She could taste the wine from earlier as it rose into her throat with a burning gurgle. She forced it to stop, to go away.

He lowered himself onto her, moaning as his lips formed around her turgid nipple. His tongue flicked, teeth nibbled.

Penny remained motionless, like a corpse.

Charlie shoved her, bounced her. Tried to rattle a response from her. But she focused on the ceiling, until Charlie's head came back into view. He looked down at her, eyes narrowed to slits and his chin jutting.

"You're gonna get it now, bitch."

He rammed into her. The girth of his erection stretched her. She felt something tear as the full length of him crammed deep. She released an involuntary squeak of pain. Charlie heard it and laughed. He began to thrust.

Penny jerked and bounced, gritting her teeth to hold in her cries. She kept her unblinking eyes locked on Charlie now, gazing deep into his. One thing she'd always admired about him had been his eyes, how they were the color of chocolate. Now they made her sick. She wanted to pluck them out and make him eat them.

Charlie kept going, swelling inside her. His hands gripped her breasts, squeezing them hard enough that she felt the pull in her shoulder blades.

He's almost done. He's almost there.

The crown on her back tooth cracked under the pressure of gritting her teeth. Charlie's thrusts became harder, faster jabs. Drool stretched down from the corner of his mouth, tapping the tip of her nose. It broke loose, splashing her face. Then it slid down, dropping into the valley at the corner of her eye.

Finally, Charlie started pumping hot thickness inside her. He twitched and shook, almost growling as his release filled her.

Spent, he collapsed on her, pinning her underneath his panting weight. After a few minutes, he'd finally caught his breath again. His head lifted. His face was scarlet under the layer of perspiration. He gave her a goofy smile.

"Thank you for your service," he said, then slapped her breasts.

The steeled armor she'd covered herself with broke, and she began to cry. The stinging sensation flowed from her breasts down to her stomach, bringing with it the shame and hurt of everything that he'd done to her.

Charlie, laughing, crawled backwards off the bed. He stood up, sighing. His shiny penis was already softening, drooping over his retracted balls like a dead snake. "I knew I'd break you. You ain't so tough. The way you are in those movies, it's like you're damn superhuman or some shit. But you're just like every other whore I've shoved my cock into. Worthless. Only a hole for me to nut in. And you all cry when I'm done with you." He stuck out his bottom lip and pretended to whimper. "Crying whores."

Penny could no longer make out the shape of him through her tears. She sniffled, trying to catch control of herself again, but it was a feeble try. She hated that he was seeing this, hated herself for breaking down in front of him.

Damn it. Alex had trained her better than this.

But not for this reason. Not for this!

"Tommy!" Charlie yelled.

The door opened. "Yes, sir?"

"Want a go at her?"

There was a pause, then Tommy said, "Really?"

"Yes, really. Do you or not?"

"I'd love one."

Penny went tight and sick inside.

Charlie laughed again. "I thought you might. Have at her. She's good shit."

"I can tell. Um, sir?"

"What?"

"Is there a way we can roll her over?"

"What the hell for?"

"I want to fuck her ass."

Charlie whistled. "I knew you were a freak. The quiet ones always are." He clapped once. "Sure thing, deputy. We'll roll her over. And when you're done, I just might have a go at that nice ass myself."

Both men laughed now.

While Penny continued to sob, she heard the clinking sound of Tommy's belt unbuckling.

Faint light began to bleed through the dark shutters of Penny's mind. Opening her eyes again, she saw faint sunlight spilling through the wispy curtains. It spread a comforting glow through the murky light of the room, beginning the cleansing that would wash away the night.

On her stomach, Penny managed to lift her head. She was alone in the room. Stretched out over the center of the bed, her ass hung off the edge, throbbing all the way through to her stomach. Tommy had gotten her first. While Charlie cheered him on, Tommy shoved harder and harder. The pain had been awful. She could tell she'd started bleeding at some point, which only seemed to excite the deputy even more.

When he finished, Charlie had his second turn. He'd been even rougher than the first time, reaching over her shoulders to grip her neck and choke her. He'd pulled her up, forcing her to arch her back while his hands squeezed so hard that she worried he might crush her esophagus. When he finally got to his second release of the night, he didn't release her throat. He held her there, bent back, her chin on his thumbs as he choked her. She'd wanted to breathe, but her lungs couldn't find any oxygen. Her vision turned splotchy at first, then went dark.

And now she was trying to swallow. Her aching throat felt too dry, and her neck felt as if it had been rung. Her arms, stretched out before her, were tied at the wrists again, but now the other end of the itchy rope had been led under the bed where it had been tied off somewhere. Whenever she tried to relax her legs, the rope tugged at her hands, burning her skin.

How long had she been in this position?

Hours.

She hurt all over. Where there wasn't pain, there was a worrying numbness. Her hands were turning blue from the rope cutting off the circulation. But right now, she couldn't care less. She wanted to know where her daughters were.

Tilting her head, she listened for any sounds. She heard nothing but the whistling melodies of birds outside.

What had they done to them? Did Charlie move on from her and go after them? Picturing him doing what he'd done to her to Ashley and Anna started a small fire in her chest that quickly spread, turning into an inferno under her skin.

I have to get loose.

She started working her wrists.

Well, that had been the plan. Her hands only hung limply, fingers loose. The commands from her brain were getting lost somewhere in her arms and not reaching the hands.

But her legs seemed okay. Sore from hanging off the other side of the bed, but okay. She put weight on her feet and nearly screamed at the aching jolt in her rump. It was the same kind of sting that came when a scab ripped open. She felt warm trickles of blood between her buttocks.

"Muh-Mom...?"

Penny froze at the scratchy sound of Anna's voice. She tried to look over her shoulder but couldn't get her arms to move enough. "Baby? Is that you?"

"Mom..." Anna's words turned thick as she started to cry.

Penny felt a surge of hope flow through her. Somehow, Anna had gotten free. "Come untie me. Quick..."

"She can't," said Charlie.

As Anna continued to sob, Penny's hope leaked from her, taking what remained of her strength. She dropped her head on the bed.

"I take back what I said earlier," said Charlie. "You're tough as shit. But your ass looks like hell." He chuckled. To Anna he said, "Come on in here."

"Leave her alone," said Penny, her mouth pressed against the mattress. "She didn't do anything."

"I already had my fun with her. I must say, the original model is way better."

He touched her.

More than touched. He hurt her. Violated her. Stole her innocence.

Penny lifted her head. "You hurt my daughter?"

"Both of them. Hell, we all did."

Penny watched as her numb hands folded into fists. "I told you what would happen if you harmed them."

"I know. And I believe you. That's why Ms. Anna here's with me. She's my insurance policy. Untie her, Trent."

"Yes, sir."

A chubby young man came around to the front of her. His hair was shaved on the sides, leaving a wide strip of cropped hair on top. He'd been one of the quiet ones at the gas station.

"You try anything," said Charlie, "and Ms. Anna gets a bullet."

"What are you doing to us now?" Penny asked.

While Trent started working at the rope on her wrists, Charlie laughed. "Just going downstairs. Ashley is already down there waiting for us. We also have a guest."

The rope fell away from her hands. At first, they remained numb. Then they began to throb as it felt like broken glass pumped through them. "What…guest?" She pulled her arms back to her, moaning at the tight knots in her shoulders.

"The boss."

Trent gripped her arm and pulled her up. He'd already untied her ankles without her noticing. On her feet, she swayed. Charlie stood behind Anna. He'd put his uniform back on at some point. Anna was wearing her long T-shirt. The collar had been stretched out, hanging low enough that her wounded shoulder was exposed. She saw teeth marks making a bruised ring on her skin under the bandage Penny had put on her. Her eyes were puffy and red, her lips chapped. Blood had dried on her chin and cheek.

"Oh, baby," said Penny, stepping forward.

"Stop," said Charlie, putting the barrel of his gun under Anna's chin. "This ain't the time for sweet embraces."

Penny wanted to hold her daughter so badly that she began to tremble. Anna stared back, tears leaking from her eyes.

"It's going to be okay, baby," said Penny.

Anna's mouth quivered. She looked at the floor.

"Don't lie to the poor girl," said Charlie. "She's been through enough. Get dressed."

Trent held out a silky bundle toward her. Penny didn't bother to ask why. She took her thin pajamas from the younger man and started putting them on. She almost fell more than once, which elicited laughter from their captors. But she stayed on her feet. It took more work than she'd expected, but she finally finished. Her fingers had cooperated a little bit, but they still felt stiff and fuzzy.

"Good," said Charlie, smiling. "Look at us. All dressed up in our Sunday finest. Now, don't you bitches go embarrassing me in front of the boss. Come on."

Charlie stayed beside Anna, keeping the gun pointing at her face. "You go down first, Trent. Keep Penny close. She's tricky."

"Yes, sir."

Even if Penny wanted to risk disobeying Charlie's orders, she didn't feel strong enough to try. Walking felt strange, as if she were inexperienced with it. Her legs were wobbly, each step causing pain.

They reached the bottom floor and made their way into the living room. The first thing Penny saw was Ashley sitting on the couch, hugging herself. She still had on Penny's robe, but it hung open low on her chest, showing most of both breasts. The slopes were dotted with purple bruises. More bruises were on her face. Her bottom lip was swollen. She turned as she heard them enter the room.

Penny expected her to say something, or to at least look happy to see her. But she only lowered her head and stared at nothing.

Penny's heart shattered.

Tommy stood over by the stone fireplace with his arms crossed. Another young man in a deputy uniform stood by the window, gazing out as if keeping watch. His hair, cut short and parted on the side, made him look more like a youth pastor than a deputy. Penny recognized him. He was the other guy at the gas station who'd help carry Levi back to the truck.

"How we doing, Eric?"

The one by the window nodded. "Good, sir. Nobody's out there."

"Don't think there will be, but you never know."

"Yes, sir."

"Sit down, darlin'," said Charlie. He shoved Anna onto the couch. She fell against Ashley, who acted as if she didn't even notice.

Penny was about to say something about his handling of her daughters.

Another voice cut her off. "Charlie. I told you, I don't like to see how you mishandle women. What you do when I'm not around is fine. But *don't* do it in front of me."

Charlie paled. He nodded. "My apologies."

Penny turned toward the sound of the woman's voice. Her aunt's recliner was turned slightly away, only revealing a pair of bare muscular legs tucked into leather boots, crossed at the knee. The skin was so smooth it looked as if she'd dipped them in clear wax.

The chair slowly spun around, showing Penny the rest of the body that was attached to the legs. She wore a pair of tight leather shorts, and a sleeveless top that could have been vinyl supported her breasts. Her black hair hung on her shoulders, silky and shiny. Her face was still lovely and much healthier than the last time Penny had seen her, except for the pale scar on her cheek that reached down from her eye to her jawline.

"Penny. You look like you've seen a ghost."

Penny had seen one. The woman she was looking at was supposed to be dead.

She'd killed Vanessa Crowe herself, many years ago.

"I've dreamed of his moment so many times," said Vanessa.

So have I. Too many times.

In Penny's dreams, she doesn't throw Vanessa's body into the ravine, watching her flailing body shrink as she plunges far below. Vanessa somehow recovers, gets the upper hand, and uses her own machetes against her.

Penny usually woke up just as the blades started to pierce her skin.

Vanessa frowned. "Where're your machetes?"

Penny stared at her, unable to find her voice.

Smiling, Vanessa said, "I know it's a lot to take in. Kind of like one of our movies, huh? You leave me for dead, and here I am years later, ready to pay you back."

"What's she talking about, Mom?" asked Anna, her voice shaky.

Vanessa looked at Anna. "Your sweet mother tried to kill me."

Anna gasped.

"Don't talk to my daughter. Talk to me."

"Still a tough bitch, huh? Tough bitch with a mouth."

"A mouth that bites, apparently," said Charlie.

"Shut up," said Vanessa.

Charlie nodded.

"You haven't told your girls that you're a killer?"

"*You're* the killer," said Penny. "You killed Alex." Both of Penny's girls gasped. In the corner of her eye, she could see their heads turning.

"I didn't want to," said Vanessa, lifting her shoulders in a slight shrug. "But…okay, I'm lying. I wanted to. He deserved it for getting you involved in the business. If he hadn't brought you in, then everything would've been just fine. *Lady Striker* would've kept going until *I* was ready for it to stop."

Penny felt tempted to, once again, argue against Vanessa's accusation that she'd been responsible for her career ending. Penny hadn't done it. Vanessa had done it to herself. But now wasn't the time to say anything at all about it.

Vanessa stood up. She turned around, taking in the room. Her mouth bent downward as she nodded. "Nice place. This would've been a great location for a movie."

Penny had thought the same thing many years ago. She'd even been tempted to pitch it to the producers of the *Machete Mama* series. But her aunt would've never agreed to it. She'd hated Penny, hated that she'd left home. Hated the movies she starred in. Hated Alex. She even hated the girls.

"I didn't really get to appreciate it the last time I was here," said Vanessa. "But now I see why you led me here those years ago. Lots of places for you to hide a body. Just like you tried you to do with mine by letting the streams carry it away. You should've used your machete to cut off my head. I wouldn't be standing here now. Charlie over there wouldn't have found me."

Penny tried to hide the shock she felt, but failed.

Charlie laughed. "If I wouldn't have been camping out there, you probably would've died. It was…meant to be."

Vanessa smirked. "It was the ancient ones, guiding me to salvation."

"And I was your savior."

"Don't say that shit," said Vanessa. "It sounds hokey when you talk like that." She stood up, her outfit making popping sounds with her movements.

"Of course. Sorry."

"Charlie, being the perverted leach that he is, kept me hidden in his house. He thought he had himself a sex slave. I played along while he nursed me back to health, letting him think he was in control. But were you in control, Charlie?"

Charlie suddenly looked like that same kid Penny had known in school. Genuine fear and embarrassment showed on his face. "No."

"Were you *ever* in control?"

"No."

"Good boy. I'd originally planned to cut off his dick and make him eat it for all the times he'd used it on me. All the times he'd brought these boys to his house and charged them money to get off on me. I let it happen for months as a plan began to manifest. I learned he was the sheriff of the town. And not only that, he knew you. He hated you as well. I used that. Of course, I had to kick the living hell out of him a bunch of times for all the things he did to me. Then I whooped all their asses, too. Right fellas?"

Tommy, Trent, and Eric agreed without much enthusiasm.

"When I was locked in Charlie's basement all that time, I realized that I could use the boys to get you. You'd gone off the radar again, so I figured they'd have the ability to track you down. Then I thought, 'Why am I thinking so small?' Charlie already had a nice side hustle in the drug trade. He ran this town. Everybody feared him. So, naturally, I took it from him. I stay out of sight, in the shadows, and Charlie does what I tell him to do, and oversees the dirty work. We've taken over this area and have started moving in on other territories."

"Damn right," said Charlie.

"And while we did that, I planned. Not only was I going to kill you. I was going to kill where you grew up. I remembered how you used to talk about this town. Made this place sound like something from an old sitcom. All those crew members would be gathered around you and Alex like little children, hearing stories about Santa Claus. You missed the town, but didn't think you'd ever come back because of your aunt. Well, I handled your aunt for you. And now you're back."

Penny felt as if she'd been punched in the stomach. "What'd you say?"

"It's easy getting away with killing someone when you run the sheriff's department."

"You killed Aunt Kathy?"

"Yeah. Drowned her in the bathtub like a sick cat. And I made sure she signed everything over to you first, promising that she'd get to live if she did. Made her believe it was you who'd sent me to do it. And let me tell you, if you thought she hated you before." Vanessa whistled. "You should've heard what she had to say about you after I told her that."

Penny balled up inside. Aunt Kathy would've believed every untrue word Vanessa said. She always accused Penny of never caring about anybody other than herself. Said she'd left the town and hoped it died, said she hoped Kathy died too. That wasn't true. She didn't like to be in the town because it reminded her of how things had been when her parents were alive. How it could never be that way again. She couldn't stand it anymore. She had to get away. Had to at least give Hollywood a try. She'd dreamed about it for so long and knew that her parents would've wanted her to give acting a shot.

They never got to see what I became, how far I went.

"You didn't come to town for the funeral, which surprised me," said Vanessa. "I was set to put my plan into motion then, but you didn't show. I started to think you wouldn't come back at all. So, I had to lure you back by thinking you were going to sell this place." Vanessa laughed. "See? I run everything. Nothing goes on here without me knowing about it."

This is all my fault.

Penny knew, somewhere in her jumbled brain, she could figure out how inaccurate that thought had been. But right now, it was all she could focus on.

She'd wanted to get Vanessa away from her girls after Alex's murder, so she'd tricked her into thinking she was coming out here to visit her aunt. She'd known Vanessa would've followed her to finish what she'd started when she'd killed Alex. Nobody else had known she'd come back to her hometown all those years ago, not even the girls. They were still so young. She'd even kept the truth about their father's death from them. Told them he'd died in an accident. She didn't want the police to interfere with her vengeance. It was between her and Vanessa.

Penny had set the trap. And Vanessa walked right into it.

And by doing that, I brought her here to become…whatever she is now.

"Vanessa," said Penny. "Just kill me and be done with it. Leave my girls out of it. They had nothing to do with anything. It's me. All me. Take your hate out on me."

"Oh, I plan to. But you need to understand something. Vanessa died that night on the mountain when you gave me this." She pointed at the thin white scar on her face. "When you address me, you address me by my *real* name." Vanessa smiled. "Lady Striker."

The men in the room began to cheer.

"You're insane," said Penny.

Vanessa giggled. "Maybe." She walked over to the fireplace. Tommy saw her coming and stepped away. Reaching the mantle, Vanessa turned and faced Penny again. "Or maybe I've just accepted who I was always meant to be. And now it's time for you to accept who you are—Machete Mama."

"I am *not* Machete Mama. I'm Penny Chambers. An actress."

Vanessa seemed to struggle with keeping her smile. "I see. That's what you're sticking with? Boring Penny Chambers. So be it. I thought Alex's death would've been enough tragedy for your true origin story. But no. I think you'll need more traumatic experiences. I think you need to lose—"

Vanessa's words were cut off by her sudden grunt. Reaching up to her head, she stumbled forward and revealed Anna standing behind her, holding a fire poker.

She looked at Penny, smiling. "Mom!"

At some point, she'd taken the poker from the stand near the couch. Penny had no clue how nobody had noticed her youngest daughter sneaking over there or creeping up behind Vanessa. Nor did she care. It was the distraction Penny had needed.

Penny sprinted the short distance between her and Vanessa. Her body felt heavier than normal, sluggish, and weighted down by the aches and hurts. But she forged ahead, bringing up her fists to finish off Vanessa before Charlie or the others decided to shoot them.

Vannesa, hunched over, suddenly turned just as Penny was about to strike. She saw the sai clutched in her fist, the twin guard tines curving on either side of her hand as the shaft protruded from between her fingers like an additional appendage. Then it was slashing through the air, tearing through her delicate shirt. A line of fire appeared up her stomach, cutting through her naval. Vanessa threw her knee up as Penny folded over, catching her under the chin. Teeth clacking together, her vision flashed. She went down to her knees, catching herself with one arm. The room swayed and tilted.

Anna screamed. Penny whipped her head around. Vanessa clutched a handful of Anna's hair as she put her face close to Anna's. "What the hell do you think you're doing, Anna?" Vanessa's words spat through her clenched teeth. She looked around at the men. "You idiots! Fucking dumbasses! None of you saw her?"

Charlie held up his hand as if he was going to speak, but never said anything.

Eric cleared his throat. "I was keeping watch on the window and…" He stopped talking.

Vanessa pulled Anna around, twisting her head so much that her ear was almost flush with her shoulder. "Just like your damn mother! Always sneaking! Always trying to stab somebody in the back!"

Penny was kicked in the side. She fell over, groaning as she tried to breathe. Her ribs felt as if they'd been pushed together. She made a mewling sound when she tried to speak.

Vanessa put the tip of the sai to Anna's throat. Her mouth stretched to show all her teeth. "I should ram this sai down your throat, Anna. Make you gargle on it! But I have plans for you. So young. People would pay top dollar for teenager. All these sick fucks around here would do anything to get between your legs. Get your shoulder patched up, get your sweet ass primed and ready."

Penny tried to shout, but all she managed to produce was a low moan.

Anna's body shook from her sobs. "Get away from me!"

Penny rolled over, pushing herself up. Vanessa saw her and kicked her in the same spot on her side again. It felt like her insides might've ruptured. The pain was crippling, bringing her back down to the floor and keeping her there. She reached out, clutching Vanessa's boot. It felt slippery in her hold.

Vanessa looked down at Penny. Her grin looked maniacal. "She's *my* little girl now. But I don't need the older sister hanging around and making things weird." She looked over at Penny's oldest daughter on the couch. Tommy stood close to her, with Trent on the other side. Ashley's face was a shiny mask of dripping tears.

Penny realized what was about to happen. "Nuh…" She shook her head, gripped Vanessa's ankle harder. "No…"

"Sorry, Ash," said Vanessa. "You're no longer needed." She held up the sai and threw it. It cut through the air with a whistling shriek that ended when the shaft punched into Ashley's chest, just below her throat.

12

Anna's screams shook the walls. "Ashley!"

Penny couldn't scream from the cramp she felt in her lungs. Instead, she moaned and squeezed Vanessa's boot. Ashley had dropped back against the couch cushion, her stiff arms bent at her sides. Her hands, locked into claws, twitched. Shock had frozen her face. The robe had fallen open. Her breasts were slicked in blood underneath the jutting handle of the sai.

She turned blurry in Penny's eyes, the horrible image saturated with her tears. When she blinked them away and looked again, Ashley was no longer twitching. Her arms had dropped onto the couch. But her eyes remained open, stuck in the ultimate moments of her terror.

"Take her," said Vanessa, flinging Anna against Charlie.

Wrapping his arms around her, he pulled her close to him. "Back together, honey."

"Shut up, Charlie," said Vanessa. She looked down at Penny again, shook her head. "Pathetic." She pulled her boot away from her hand. Her fingers made tapping sounds on the floor from her shakes. "I have fantasized about this moment for years. *Years!* And you've *ruined* it for me. You've gone weak. Your strength used to be in your unpredictable methods. There's nothing mysterious about you anymore. You're…just a mom. Not a machete mama. Just a normal, puny mama. And it saddens me. I wanted to earn your death. I wanted to fight for it, how we were trained. Now, it just feels like a mercy kill. Putting an old dog out of its misery because nobody wants to take care of it anymore."

Crouching, Vanessa caressed Penny's cheek. She moved her hand under her chin and pulled upward. Penny had no choice but to follow her lead and get onto her knees. She looked at Vanessa through her teary eyes. She looked smudged, a watercolor painting that was smearing on the canvas.

"Such a waste," said Vanessa.

"Mom!"

Anna's voice broke through the surrender she'd accepted inside, shattering the defeat and heartache that had fallen over her like a dome.

Ashley was gone, but Anna still needed her.

She needs me to fight.

Just as she'd done with Charlie earlier, she shot her head forward. Their foreheads collided with a dull *thonk*. Vanessa uttered a grunt and staggered back in a reverse crab walk before dropping onto her ass.

"Shit!" Charlie yelled from somewhere behind her. "I should've warned you about that damn head of hers!"

Dazed, Penny got to her feet. Her vision couldn't settle. It broke apart, separating the room as if it had mirrored itself. There were two Vanessas rising to her feet, side by side, connected at their elbows.

Penny, bringing up her fists, took a step forward. Her toe bumped against a piece of iron.

The poker.

Sticking her toes under the bar, she lifted her leg and brought the poker into the air. Her two right arms reached out, catching both pokers at the same time. When she blinked, her vision reconnected, and she caught Vanessa running at her, brandishing another sai. She jabbed. The sai's point came at her face. Penny dipped to the side, brought up the poker, and whacked Vanessa's stomach. Air shot out of her mouth as she bent over the bar.

Penny twisted the bar around, then yanked it back. The sharp tooth under the tip slashed across Vanessa's midriff, slicing her top open. Her skin showed in the gap, filling with red as the wound began to bleed. Penny could tell it wasn't a major hit, but she still felt a twinge of delight because she'd hurt the bitch. She swung the poker upward, hoping to lodge the sharp tooth dripping Vanessa's blood in her throat.

Vanessa jumped back, momentarily using the recliner for support as she flipped over to the other side. The men cheered again, obviously impressed.

"I love watching her do that shit!" Trent yelled.

Penny didn't waste time. She chased after her, leaping onto the seat. The recliner tipped, the back of the chair going to the floor. Vanessa came out from behind it, thrusting the sai. Penny cartwheeled over Vanessa's arm to more cheers, missing the blade but not the tine. It raked her forearm, tearing her skin open with hot pain.

Her bare feet smacked the floor. As she started to turn, Vanessa stepped close, bringing the sai with her. Turning her hand, she rammed the pommel into Penny's stomach. The round end of the handle hit the slash that was already there, spreading it wider. Penny's wounded scream nearly drowned out Anna's worrisome cries.

Vanessa yanked the sai away, spun on her heel, and kicked Penny in the back of the head. The impact threw Penny toward Eric, where he stood by the window. He jumped out of the way right before Penny bounced off the wall. Staggering back, Penny caught a glimpse of Vanessa's shadow shift across the wall. She was behind her, about to attack. Dropping into a split, both legs straight out on each side, her crotch touched the floor. She looked up, seeing the sai shoot through the space her head had just been a split second before.

"Holy shit!" Charlie yelled. "Look at that split!"

Vanessa's head appeared in Penny's vision, gazing down as her raven-black hair curtained her face. She swung down with the sai. Penny pulled her legs around, rolled back, and missed the tip of the sai another time. It scuffed the floor, knocking out a chunk of wood.

Vanessa, crouched on the floor, laughed. "This is what I wanted! Fight for your life, bitch!" Jumping to her feet, she ran and leapt onto the coffee table, throwing herself into the air again and flipped. She landed in front of Penny, bringing the sai down in a smooth motion.

Her technique has improved.

Penny blocked the attack with the poker. The connecting metal clamored. The vibrations moved up Penny's arm, triggering the slash near her biceps to throb again. She dropped the poker and caught it with her other hand.

Then she screamed when the sai shot through her forearm. The shaft was doused in blood.

Vanessa, still gripping the handle, hooted. She yanked forward, wrenching Penny's arm away from her body. She gave Penny's chest three quick stiff kicks. The poker rattled when it hit the floor. Penny hadn't even noticed she dropped it again. She couldn't feel her hand.

"Leave my mom alone!"

Vanessa laughed. "She's got that spunk you used to have, Penny."

She flipped the sai, held it by the blade, and swung it. The pommel whacked Penny above the ear. Everything went black, then slowly came back through the splotches and static. Her ears were ringing. She even felt pulsations in her teeth.

She looked over and saw Ashley on the couch. Her head was tilted back against the cushions, mouth slack. The other sai still stuck up from her chest. Penny's eyes kept turning and found Anna. Trapped in Charlie's hold, her mouth was moving as she shouted something that Penny couldn't understand through the loud feedback droning in her head.

It looked like she was trying to warn her about something.

As Penny started to wonder what it was, she felt a poke in her back. A cold hardness went through her chest. Her silky tank top bulged, then split open as the sai's blade ripped through.

Penny had never felt such pain. It took over everything—her insides, her reflexes, her thoughts. Gone were the worries and grief about her daughters, gone was the anger and hate she felt for Vanessa and the deputies in the living room. All that was left was the agony that had paralyzed her.

Yet, she was moving somehow. Penny didn't know how it had happened, but she was off the floor and floating toward the window. The realization, albeit faint, that she was being carried blinked somewhere in the fog shrouding her brain. She jerked to a halt, then slid forward, gliding off the sai's shaft. Her feet managed to get underneath her, bracing her as she stumbled toward the window. Bringing up her hand, she caught herself on the glass just before slamming against it.

She started to turn around. Vanessa was there, rushing with the sai. It sliced down her chest, dissecting her top and the flesh underneath. Blood jumped from the horizontal gash in a spraying line. The additional pain pushed against her consciousness, threatening to take it away. Her vision faded, losing the vivid colors, going gray and bleak.

Vanessa stepped forward and rammed the sai into Penny's stomach. Penny went rigid. Her breath snagged in her chest. Somehow, she could taste the cold steel. It coated the back of her throat and filled her mouth.

Vanessa leaned in, breathing on Penny's face. "Finally. *I* can be at peace." She looked down for a moment. When she looked into Penny's eyes again, she was grimacing. "Get off my sai." She shoved.

Penny's back hit the window. The glass shattered behind her, taking away the support.

With nothing behind her, she dropped.

The darkness was pacifying. Painless. She felt nothing in the empty silence, which had become so soothing since the pain had ravished her.

She remembered everything. The memory of Ashley's death and her own came to her in sparks of brutal images. She'd been on the ground, on her stomach. Bloody and dying.

And they'd come outside, laughing. Charlie held her up while Trent and Tommy took turns punching her in the face and stomach. The face hits had hurt, but whenever she took one in the stomach, their fists managed to pound the sai wounds. Blood sprayed. The pain was unlike anything she'd ever felt before.

When they were finished with her, she was still conscious. On the ground, she moaned. That was when Lady Striker had come outside. The last thing Penny remembered was Vanessa's thick boot filling her vision.

Then the black had taken her, covered her, wrapped her in its numbing void. An obsidian cocoon that she never wanted to leave.

"Penny?"

Though she was not physical, she could somehow see the darkness, could hear her name emanating from the emptiness.

And the voice was one she'd missed so much. Though she had no eyes, she felt tears begin to fall.

"Alex?"

"It's me."

"I've missed you so, so much."

"I've missed you, too, baby."

"I need you…"

"You've given up," he said in a said voice.

"Yuh-yes…"

"Why?"

"I lost."

"You lost the battle. Not the war. You have to get up."

"I can't. I want to come home. To you."

She could see him now, detached from the darkness. His presence was a shimmering glow, an outline of soothing light. He was translucent, a hologram projected against nothing. But he looked perfect. He felt perfect. His warmth reached her, embraced her like one of his hugs. "I want you to come home too." His smile was warm. "But you can't. Not yet. You're too early."

Penny felt more tears welling. "Why can't I? I'm here now. Please. Let me…"

"Anna needs you."

Anna.

Where *was* Anna?

"I can't do it," said Penny. "I can't fight anymore."

"Like before, you've already accepted your defeat before you began to fight."

"I can't beat her. She's better than me."

"She was never better than you. Even now. Not in her abilities. Not in her heart, mind, and spirit. You are superior to her. She knows it. And she's afraid. She used the darkness to hide in. It's consumed her. It's always had its hold on her."

"I made her that way. I did that."

"She was born that way. You have always been stronger."

"You're wrong," said Penny. "You were always wrong about me. I'm weak."

"You're weakened. Not weak. Complacent. You're asleep inside. The drive within you is dormant. You need to get up, wake it up. And *fight*."

Penny shook her head. She wanted to believe it was that simple, wanted him to be right. But she knew he wasn't. She was the same timid Penny she'd been before she'd ever met Alex Chambers. He'd just given her the tools to hide it better.

But no. That doesn't sound right.

Had she not discovered who she truly was when she began training? Didn't she finally feel alive, as if she was finally doing what she'd been put here to do?

"Mom?"

Ashley stood beside her father, a luminous representation of herself. Her hair flowed around her beautiful face like water. Her eyes were bright and full of vivid life. No longer were they wide and white and soulless. Here, she was alive and full of vitality.

"My baby," said Penny. "I'm so sorry I couldn't...save you. I tried...I..."

Ashley tilted her head, letting the rippling hair hang like a waterfall. "I'm okay, Mom. I'm at peace here with Daddy. It's Anna who needs your help."

"Anna will die if you don't get up," said Alex.

"I can't feel my body."

"You're out of your body. You're in the realm between living and the dead. You can't go any further. Because you're not supposed to. You have to turn around and go back."

"I want to be with you. Both of you."

"Then who will be with Anna?"

Penny felt ashamed for not thinking of Anna. "I can't beat Vanessa, Alex. I told you, I can't!"

"She is not Vanessa Crow anymore," said Alex. "She's truly become Lady Striker. She has spit on the teachings of the ancient ones, twisted the arts for her own warped desires. You knew her like I did. She was always a disgrace to the craft. Abusing her status, abusing her power and influence. She was a student of the dark way before you ever threw her off the mountain. What was left of her died that night. But what remained was even worse."

"You have to be Machete Mama now," said Ashley. "You can't be Penny Chambers. You can't be…Mom."

"That's all I am now," said Penny. "That's all that's left. Vanessa didn't die alone on that mountain. Machete Mama died with her."

"She's sleeping, like I said," said Alex. "She's buried but not dead. Like you. She needs to be reborn. You allowed Machete Mama to take over that night. You need to let her come back. Give her life again. She *is* you. And *you must* save Anna."

"And avenge us," said Ashley. She had Ashley's voice, her face, but the words coming from the entity that looked like her daughter came from somebody else.

Penny knew the words were old as time.

Wrongs needed to be righted.

Vengeance needed to be inflicted.

Bloody vengeance. Violent retaliation.

For her family.

"You need to wake up now," said Alex. "Now's not the time for us all to be together again. You have to heal. You have to save our little girl."

"And kill Lady Striker," said Ashley. "For good."

"For good," said Penny. Alex was fading from her sight, but his warmth remained, flowing through her. She felt it all over, returning strength to her. Not all of it, but it would be enough for now.

"Wake up," said Alex. "If you don't wake up now, it'll be too late. Your window is closing."

Penny heard a scraping sound, followed by a thick *clop* above her. It repeated, over and over, blended with a steady hissing sound.

Not hissing…rain…

Though Penny was still covered by darkness, she could feel again and wished she couldn't. The agony was almost its own living thing, tormenting her as the weight from above became heavier with each plopping sound.

There were unfamiliar voices, two of them, muffled above her.

Move.

It was her voice and somehow Alex's voice mended together.

You're running out of time.

Penny tried to lift her arms. They were weighed down on either side of her. She couldn't move at all. Even breathing was impossible from the mushy compression against her face. It felt cold on her cheeks, filling her nostrils with an earthy smell as the squishy solidity pressed her down more and more.

I'm being buried.

That was why Alex said she was running out of time. If she didn't start fighting her way out from the sodden earth, she would be trapped there, slowly suffocating during her final breaths.

No!

Penny shook her shoulders, wiggling herself bit by bit. As the mud began to shift, more slid into the loose spots, compacting her tighter. Realizing this was happening made her thrash even more. Her knees pushed against the soggy ground, lifting it. More oozed down, pressing into weaker spots like wet cement.

She was starting to panic, to lose all control. She was better than this. She'd never free herself if she let her emotions guide her. Doing so would only get her killed. Her mind was the strongest part of her. And it controlled everything else. The rest of her body obeyed her mind, and Penny was in control of her mind once again.

Alex had taught her how to slow her heartbeat, how to let her mind flow without her conscience interfering. Her own instincts would know what to do when she couldn't comprehend any course of action herself.

And it did. Her body began to move. Not in wild bursts of fear like it had been, but smooth slithers of her arms, worming their way through the mud. They pushed into the thick pastiness, bending to form traction. Then she hefted herself. Her back lifted, sliding upward through shifting mud. Soon, her face was touching her hands. She almost lost herself with a premature celebration. She wasn't there quite yet. Though the ground above her felt shallow and pliable now, she could still mess this up.

Her feet had to get underneath her. This would be harder, but still doable. She would have to take her time. Her lungs continued to expand like a balloon filling with heat. Soon they would pop. If she didn't get her head above the ground, she would be forced to breathe. Air wouldn't be sucked into her chest, only thick, clumpy mud.

There!

Penny's legs were under her. Her arms were reaching out to either side as she crouched under the soil. Now it was time to stand up.

Straining, Penny shoved upward, working from her knees. The ground weighing on her shoulders began to fall away as she rose. Rain pelted the top of her head and her shoulders. It flowed down her, washing away the mud as she clambered out of the ground.

Daylight had replaced the night. Gray daylight hidden under thick layers of dark clouds. Her eyes still ached, as if a spotlight had been pointed at her face.

She pushed down on the mushy ground, hands sinking as she hoisted the rest of herself out of the ground. Landing on her side, she rolled away from the hole she'd made. The rain pounded down on her, each droplet feeling like a rock when it struck her aching skin.

She tilted back her head and let the rain fill her mouth. She swallowed. The rain was cold and good as it cleansed her dry throat. More flowed into her nostrils. She blew out clumps of dirt, opening her nose to breathe again.

She heard those voices again, floating through the pouring rain. Close but starting to fade.

Penny took a deep breath, then sat up. The pain felt like it might make her black out. Two men stood off to the side, wearing clear rain slickers. One had a shovel, stabbed into the ground, while gripping the top. The other shorter man was just starting to say something about leaving his shovel by the hole. He was starting to turn around. Soon as he did, he would see Penny.

But that was okay. Because Penny had already found the shovel. It was on the ground in front of her.

She grabbed the shovel and jumped to her feet. Her feet dug into the mud as she rushed the man. Her vision blurred more than once, threatening her with passing out. It was more exerting crossing the short distance than it should have been. But she was injured, near death, and the ground was like oatmeal. Yet, even with all that working against her, she still reached the men just as the shorter one was starting to face her.

He saw her and yelled. Then the shovel blade smashed into his open mouth, slicing his cheeks. The tip came out through the back of his head. She shoved the long handle down, removing the rest of his head away from the jaw and neck. Blood came with it, splashing Penny with warmth that the rain quickly rinsed away.

The taller man was now also screaming. "How? You were dead! You..." Penny hit his face with the flat side of the shovel. There was a vibrating clang, and the man flew back. His back smacked the mud.

Penny got down beside him, shoving a bare knee into the mud. She looked down, noticing for the first time that her pajama top was gone. All she had on were the silk shorts. And they were stained from blood and dirt. Her torso was a map of wounds. Her belly was open like a crooked mouth. The two holes from the sai blades were hollow eyes on either side above the gaping slit. Her forearm had a single cavity that went all the way through. Torn flesh rimmed the hole.

She gave the man a quick look over. He was probably around the same age as Charlie's deputies. Maybe this guy was one of them. But his rotted teeth and sunken eyes made her think that wasn't the case. Most likely, just a druggie, doing a job for Charlie to score.

"Where am I?" she asked him.

"What?"

His nose had been pushed to the side from the shovel hit. She flicked the mashed tip. The man howled as if she'd stepped on his balls. She'd do that next if he didn't answer her question.

"Don't play dumb. Where am I?"

"The...Body Farm..." he said between sobs.

The what?

Penny looked around. Flat ground stretched all around her, freshly plowed as if a harvest was expected to grow here. Trees bordered the far side, veiled in mist. "What do you mean by that?"

This time, the man didn't mess around. "This is where they make us bury them."

"Bury who?"

"The ones they kill. It's away from everything. Nobody comes out here."

Penny looked around again. There was a lot of land. She doubted every inch was concealing a decayed corpse, but there were probably way more than she could ever guess. She lowered her head to the man. Her drenched hair dangled by her face. "Did you bury a girl today? Younger than me."

The man nodded. "Yuh..."

Penny slapped his nose. His scream hurt her ears. Pushing her hand over his mouth, she spoke through clenched teeth. "Dig her up." The man's eyes widened. His breath fluttered against her palm. "You heard me. Dig her up. Now."

Penny sat on the ground, hunched over and covering her wounds with her hands while the man dug next to the spot Penny had been buried. The rain made his work harder and took longer than it probably would any other time. She knew this was taking time she probably couldn't spare, but she couldn't care less. She wanted Ashley out of this awful field of unmarked graves.

"Be careful you don't hurt her with the shovel."

The man paused for a second, then went back to work. A few minutes later, he said, "I found her."

Penny used the other shovel to help her stand. "Pull her out and lay her down."

The man seemed hesitant to do it at first. He glanced at Penny, thought better of it, and crouched at the edge. He reached inside the hole. As he stood, he lifted Ashley. She was caked in mud, but the rain was doing a good job of cleaning it off. She still wore the robe, though it hung open, leaving her naked body exposed to the downpour. Her eyes were still stuck open in that awful shock.

He placed her on the ground. Penny stumbled over to her, crouching. She pulled the robe shut, tying the soaked belt. Then she used her fingertips to close Ashley's eyes. She held them shut for a few seconds before removing her fingers.

"Pick her up," she said.

The man huffed. "Listen, lady. I…"

Penny stood up. "Want me to break your jaw next?"

"Nuh-no…"

"Then do what I say."

The man nodded, then did what she said. He stood there, holding Ashley as if she were his bride.

"Do you have a car?" she asked.

"A truck."

"Where?"

"Just over there."

"Anybody in it?"

"No. It was just Jay and me. We do the burying for Lady Striker."

Lady Striker.

Penny nodded. "What's your name?"

"Cleet."

"Cleet?" He nodded. "Like the shoe?" Another nod. "Jesus. Let's head to your truck."

She walked behind him through the field. The mud was like quicksand, pulling at her feet with each step she made. Sometimes it tugged her down to her knees. She pulled herself out, wincing from how the movements flared up her pains.

"I don't know how you lived through what they did to you," said Cleet. "You must be the toughest broad I've ever seen."

"Shut up."

"Okay."

Through the slashing rain torrents, Penny began to make out the pale shape of the truck. It was long, bulky, and old. Maybe it had been a tanned color at one time, but now it was the color of old dog shit and tarnished with streaks of rust.

They walked up to the clunker. Penny looked in the back. Tarps had been left in the bed. Rain had pooled in some of the creases. Most likely, Cleet and Jay had brought them here wrapped up in the blue sheets. "Put her in the back," Penny said. "Wrap her in the tarps."

While he climbed in the back of the truck and did what she said again, Penny opened the driver's side door.

Something was lying on the seat that she hadn't expected to find, but she was glad it was there.

Cleet sighed. "Done. Now I ain't takin' no more orders from you. You done kilt Jay, and Lady Striker is gonna…" He stopped talking when Penny jacked a round into the shotgun that had been on the seat. Cleet, standing higher up in the truck bed, stared down at her. "What are you doing with that?"

The rain streamed down her, dripping off the tip of the barrel. "You're right. You're not taking orders from me anymore because I'm done giving them."

"Now, wait. I did everything you said. I did it with a broke nose. My name's Cleet for Christ's sake!"

"But you work for Lady Striker. That makes you my enemy."

He shook his head. "*I'm* your enemy? I don't even know who you are!"

"I'm Machete Mama."

She pulled the trigger. The gun's kick threw her shoulder back. Cleet's stomach burst from the blast. He was thrown back, feet going high as he dropped over the other side of the truck. His body landed in the mud with a deep squelch.

Penny didn't care much for guns. She'd used them in movies from time to time. They did their job well, but she only used them as a last resort. And this was one of those times. Plus, she was too weak and tired to fight right now. The little advantage of the .12-gauge buckshot had come in handy.

Tossing away the gun, she climbed into the truck, pulled the door shut, and leaned back against the seat. It felt good to be sitting down somewhere dry. She listened to the rain's heavy tapping on the truck's roof. It was a soothing sound.

Cranking the engine, she turned the heat on. The air was cool for the first little bit, then it warmed. She leaned over, hanging her wet hair in front of the air vent. She squeezed the access wetness from her locks, relishing the warm buffets against her face.

She couldn't stay here much longer. She wasn't even sure exactly where she was. For all she knew, another twenty men had heard the gunshot and were coming for her. She doubted that was the case, though. They'd already be here by now if she had anything to worry about.

Still, she couldn't hang around. She needed to go somewhere, to get out of sight. They'd eventually figure out she was still alive. She needed to prepare.

And she knew where to go.

It had been over twenty years since Penny had been to Misty's house. The last time, Misty's parents were still alive, and the two girls had just graduated from high school. They were up in Misty's room the Saturday after the ceremony. Penny was stretched out on her side on Misty's bed while her best friend sat on the floor, showing Penny brochures that she'd snatched from the travel center in another town.

"See? Look at that *beach!* If we leave Monday, we'll have the whole week to ourselves. Nothing but sunshine and sand and cute guys in swimming trunks the whole time. We've always wanted to do that."

Penny smiled. "It would be a good time."

"Then why don't you want to go with me?"

"I *do* want to go with you. But I'm saving my money for—"

"California. Yeah. I know. But it's not like this trip will take *all* your money. I'll pay for our hotel room. My uncle gave me five hundred dollars yesterday himself. And all the other money I got, we'll be okay. Plus, my parents said they'll give us money for the trip. We'll never get an offer like this again. I start college in August, Penny. That's barely two months away. This is all the time we have left."

The pleading expression on her best friend's face made her feel awful. It would have been a great trip. Their last chance to get out and have fun together before their new lives began. But Penny wasn't going to college. She was going to LA. It had been her plan ever since her parents died in the car crash.

But by going to LA, she was abandoning the only real friend she'd ever had. Misty had become closer to her than a normal best friend. They were like sisters, and Misty's parents were like Penny's own. She cared more about them than her own aunt. And she would be leaving the whole family behind.

"I can't, Misty. I'm sorry."

Misty nodded. She looked down at the brochures. "Okay. Sure." She grabbed the folded sheets and crumpled them in her hands.

"What are you doing?"

Standing up, Misty walked over to the trash can by her desk. "What's it look like? You're not going, so what's the point of keeping them?"

"We can go another time."

"Oh, you're going to fly all the way back here, from a state surrounded by the ocean, just to go to the beach with me?"

"Sure."

"Yeah, right." Misty crossed her arms. Tapping her foot, she stood beside the trash can, staring at the wall. She took a deep breath before saying, "I think you need to leave."

Penny opened her eyes. She was on her back, staring at the ceiling. Blurry at first, it slowly came into focus. She didn't recognize the ceiling fan above her. Confused, she moved her eyes and looked at the wall. A painting hung there. Penny recognized the spot the artist had done an immaculate job of recreating in oils. It was the mountain, its peak poking through a blanket of pink mist. The sun was setting behind it, spilling a combination of gaudy shades across the top.

Where am I?

At first, she thought she was in the hospital. She could feel tape on her skin, could feel the cold touch of bandages on her injuries. But the blanket was not the same generic white style the hospitals provided. This one was covered in flowers and looked as if it was homemade. There was no antiseptic smell.

She was in somebody's bedroom.

"Oh, thank God!" The voice came from the other side of her through a loud gasp. "You lived!"

Penny turned her head. Well, that had been the plan, but its weight only tugged it in that direction and let it flop sideways. Misty sat in a chair beside the bed. She wore a jersey with 45 on the front. Reaching an inch or two down her thighs, it was green with white stripes and numbers. Her legs were bare and tanned the same dark shade as her arms and face. Her lemon-colored hair was mussed and tangled.

"Misty?" Penny's voice sounded like two stones grinding together.

Jumping to her feet, Misty rushed over to the bed. She held an object in her hand, aiming it at her forehead like a gun. There was a beep, then she pulled it away and looked at it. "Ninety-nine. Still a slight fever, but I bet it drops." She put the thermometer on the nightstand, then placed her hand on Penny's forehead. She kept it there for a moment, moving it down to Penny's cheek. "You don't feel that warm, either. That's good. The fever broke. You woke up. You're alive. The worst part's over."

Penny was about to ask more questions, but Misty distracted her with a glass of water. A crooked straw stuck up from inside. "Drink. *Don't* guzzle."

Penny noticed she was elevated, her back angled slightly upward. "Am I in the hospital?" She formed her dry lips around the straw and drank. The water was cool and refreshing.

"Easy," said Misty, pulling the glass away much too soon. "You'll make yourself sick." She put the glass on the small rolling desktop beside the thermometer. She sighed. "No. You're not in the hospital. You should be, though."

"I can't go to the hospital…"

"I know. That's all you kept saying last night when I found you on my front porch. Don't call the police. No police. No hospital. Help me. Then you passed out. I didn't think you were going to wake up."

Penny had no memory of anything beyond leaving the field where she'd been buried alive. Her plan had been to come to Misty for help. Evidently, she'd made it that far, but barely.

"You're lucky I still had mom's bed from when she couldn't walk anymore. I'd planned to get rid of it but just couldn't bring myself to do it. It's clean, though. So are the sheets. No worries there. I cleaned you up the best I could, bandaged you up. Put that diaper on you. Sorry that you're naked other than that."

Penny struggled to lift the sheets that were tucked under her chin. She saw her damaged breasts, the stark white strips of bandages on her chest and stomach breaking up the combination of purple, green, and yellow bruises on her skin. Some lighter scratches were uncovered and scabbed. The diaper was the adult variety saved for nursing home patients and the elderly. Probably left over from what she'd used on her mother during the worse days at the end.

Her eyes moved over to the arm holding the sheet. Another thick wad of gauze was wrapped around her forearm. She remembered the hole Vanessa's sai had made.

Lady Striker.

She looked at Misty. "You haven't told anybody that…"

Misty walked over to the window. She was lifting it when she looked over her shoulder. "I told you that you said not to. But I was going to anyway soon as I got you handled and made sure you were still alive. I went outside…and…saw what you had in the back of the truck."

Penny had no idea what she was talking about. What truck? Penny didn't have a truck, so how had she been driving one?

Then her mind started to show her glimpses. She'd already remembered being buried and now saw herself killing the two guys and stealing the truck.

What was in the back of the truck?

She saw Cleet lifting Ashley out of the ground, her skin covered in gloppy mud. Everything came back to her in a rush that took her breath away. "Ashley."

"That's her name?"

Penny nodded.

Misty, sitting in a wooden chair by the window, lit a cigarette. "Imagine my reaction when I found her out there."

Fresh tears filled Penny's eyes. "The truck…it needs to be…"

"Hidden? Already did that. It's in Dad's shop. I put Ashley…" Misty closed her eyes, letting smoke waft out her nostrils. When she opened them again, she said, "She's in the deep freezer. I didn't know what else to do. She had wounds like yours, and you said not to call the police, and I figured Charlie must've had something to do with it. He's a rotten bastard."

Penny felt even more drained now than she had when she first opened her eyes.

"Thank you, Misty," Misty said in a high-pitched voice. "Thank you for helping me, even though you have no idea what happened or what's going on."

Penny swallowed the dry lump in her throat. Her jaw shook. "Thank you, Misty."

"Want to tell me what the hell all this is about?"

Though Penny could vividly see it all in every morbid detail, putting everything into words was challenging. She spoke slowly, her words broken apart by whimpers and, at times, the inability to express the awful facts.

Misty gave her the space and the time she needed to sort out everything. It took a while, but she eventually got her old best friend caught up on everything that happened in the last twenty-four hours.

Wait. Has it only been that long?

Misty finished her third cigarette, then brought the glass of water to Penny. She allowed her to drink more this time and Penny was thankful. Her throat felt shredded raw from so much talking. Misty put the almost empty glass back on the rolling desktop.

"How long have I been here?" asked Penny.

Misty took a deep breath. "Four days."

Penny's instant reaction had been to sit up. She barely made it off the pillow before dropping back down.

"Easy," said Misty. "You're in no condition to move, especially fast like that."

"Four days?" said Penny. Hearing herself say it wasn't any easier than it had been hearing Misty say it.

Misty returned to the chair by the window and lit another cigarette. "From taking care of Mom for so many years, I became a pretty good nurse. Plus, all the kids' booboos at the daycare."

"Who's watching the daycare if you've been here?"

"Please. I own the place. I only go in on Fridays these days to do payroll and billing. Everything else I do from my phone. I've got good workers handling things for me."

More tears dribbled from Penny's eyes. "Thank you, Misty. I don't know what…" She sniffled, the words becoming lost behind her emotions.

"Don't thank me," said Misty. "We're all trapped under Charlie's bullshit."

Penny looked at her. She was a smeared object through her tears. "What do you mean?"

"Charlie's been running this town for a long time."

"He doesn't run it anymore."

"From what you've told me, it doesn't sound like it. And this Lady Striker is Vanessa Crowe. The actress from your movies?"

"Yeah. But she's not the same. She's…lethal."

"I can tell, if she managed to do all that to you."

A cold feeling formed deep inside Penny's stomach, causing her stab wounds to ache. "If they find out you're helping me…"

Misty held up her hand. "Let's hope they don't find out."

"We need to get rid of that truck. I'm sure they've found the bodies and know I'm not in the ground anymore."

"True. But I can handle that tonight when it's dark. I'll dump it in the quarry or something."

"You'd have to break in. Just get it away from here. I'll go with you."

"Penny. You should be dead. The fact that you aren't is a miracle of *epic* proportions. You could make a fortune telling your survival story all over the world."

Penny thought back to her book. How she'd been recounting her life story only for a new chapter to have been created in the process. A darker chapter that was only going to get darker.

Because so many people are going to die.

Penny's hands ached. Not from the leftover soreness of her last battle.

It was a craving that started in her fingers and moved through her hands. A yearning.

They wanted to hold her machetes again.

Penny had only taken a few steps before she started to fall. Thankfully, Misty had been walking with her and was able to catch her.

"See?" said Misty. "I told you this was a bad idea."

"I'm just...working out the kinks."

"Kinks my ass. You're still near death. You should be in bed, recovering. Or we could drive you to another town, check you into a hospital there, get some cops at your door, and—"

"No. Who knows how far Lady Striker's reach is? I can't risk it. It's all up to me."

"It shouldn't be," said Misty. "We can call the FBI."

"No."

Misty, an arm around her back, took slow steps to match Penny's lethargic, wobbly gait. Penny noticed that she was moving better than she had been and that her muscles didn't feel so much like dry-rotted rubber.

"You're bleeding again," said Misty. "Let's get you to the chair."

Misty helped Penny over to the chair she'd used for smoking. She eased Penny down onto the seat. Penny sighed. Only now she realized how badly she'd been sweating. Her skin was shiny with perspiration. She looked down and saw a red stain on the T-shirt Misty had loaned her to wear.

The stain was low on the shirt—her stomach.

"Hopefully you didn't tear your stitches," said Misty, almost as if she were talking to herself. She pulled up Penny's shirt, exposing her reconnected flesh to the cool air of the room.

Penny looked away after only a glimpse of the black lines tracking this way and that. She'd never seen so much thread holding flesh together.

"The stitches seem okay. It's this other gash. It wasn't bad enough for stitches but looks like it's too bad for just a bandage. I should glue it, but all I have is super glue. Not really medically approved."

"I approve it."

"I'm only pretending to be a nurse here, but even I can confidently say that's a horrible idea. The chemicals alone are—"

"Misty? Please. Don't fight me on this. Whatever it takes to make it stop bleeding. I've got a lot of work to do and not a lot of time to do it."

Misty's lips pressed into a tight line. She gave a terse nod. "Fine." She walked out of the room.

Penny felt bad now. Misty was going above and beyond the normal call of friendship to help her as much as she already had. It'd been years since they had even talked. And

Misty was treating her as if their friendship had never faltered at all through that time.

But Penny had meant what she'd said. She didn't have the time that Misty said she needed. She had to get back to training.

Misty returned with the super glue. After she removed the bandage, she pinched the flaps of skin together and dropped a gooey line in the dip. Holding it there, she counted to herself. Penny hardly even felt it. Maybe because she was so sore everywhere else.

Misty released the fold of skin. The glue held. She put another layer of glue on top of it to seal it. "That's probably the best I'll be able to get it. No more physical stuff for a bit. It needs to completely dry."

Penny nodded. "What've you got to eat in this place?"

"How can you be hungry? I was going to give you baby food."

"Ew. Why?"

"You had a sai rammed all the way through you. Twice. In your stomach."

"I think she missed my actual stomach."

Misty shook her head. "I can't believe you almost died. You're acting like you were only in a bicycling accident or something. You don't look like that, though. You look like somebody who'd almost died."

"Thanks."

"I'm talking about the wounds. You've always been gorgeous."

"You're prettier than me."

Misty's cheeks reddened. "Oh, please."

"Whatever happened between you and Garth Matthews?"

"Ugh. Garth." She rolled her eyes. "We got married."

"You did?" Penny was shocked. "When did this happen?"

"About a year after you left. He proposed that September after graduation. I'd just started school for childcare. He expected me to drop out and stay at home, but I didn't. We were doomed from the start."

"Is he still around here?"

Misty shook her head. "Moved out to Brickston, last I heard. That was years ago."

"Seeing anybody now?"

Misty's eyes clouded over for a moment. Then she gave a smile that looked forced. "Why are you so nosey?"

"That's a 'no'."

Misty gasped. "You shit. If you weren't so mangled, I'd smack you. You'd probably catch my hand, though, and do something painful to it."

Penny smiled. The tugging at the corners of her mouth felt odd, as if her face no longer knew how to form the expression. "To you? Nah."

Misty shook her head. "How'd you learn all that stuff?"

"My husband taught me."

"He taught you how to do the spiral flip thing you did in *Divide and Conquer*? Where you flipped over those two guys and kicked them both in the face at the same time?"

"Well, no, he didn't teach me *that*."

"Was it a stunt double?"

"Nope. It was me. I did all my own stunts. Alex taught me the craft, and I used it to stage out the fight scenes with others who were trained by him. Alex was a true master. A perfect human. He..." Something clicked in Penny's head. "How do you know about that scene? You've seen it?"

Misty's face went crimson again. "Uh..." She winced. "I'm embarrassed now."

"What for?"

"I'm a huge fan."

Penny laughed, then groaned at the pain. "I don't believe you."

"I'd show you, but you'd think I'm a freak."

"Oh, jeez. Seriously? Now I'm not sure I want to know."

"Now I feel like I have to show you, so you know I'm *not* some weirdo."

"I know you're a weirdo."

"Ha ha," said Misty, smirking. "I see the sense of humor you think you have is returning."

It was Penny's turn to gasp. "Hey!"

Laughing, Misty stood up. "Come on. Let me show you. Then I'll make you some soup."

"What kind?"

"Beef vegetable."

Her stomach grumbled at the mention of it. "Sounds amazing. Your mom's recipe?"

"It is. I made a huge pot yesterday. It's been sitting in the fridge for over a day. All the flavors should have soaked together just right."

"Maybe you should show me after we eat."

"We'll see it on the way. Only a short detour." She held out her hand.

Penny was about to reach for it, then stopped herself. "Let me try myself."

"Don't be stubborn. You…"

Penny stood up on wobbly legs. She swayed a few times, then seemed to be okay. "I'm all right."

"Fine."

Though the speed was almost in reverse, it was so slow, Penny made it into the hallway without any help. She leaned against the wall, panting. Sweat ran down her face. Droplets got caught in her eyelids. When she blinked, they fell away.

"Maybe I should get the wheelchair," said Misty.

"I'll be okay. I'm in control of my body."

"That's not how it works sometimes."

"It's how it has to work for me."

Misty didn't say anything else. After another minute or two, Penny felt like she could continue. She nodded.

They made their way into the living room. The wall that separated it from the kitchen had been removed at some point to make it an open area that was only divided by the couch that backed up to where the kitchen began.

"Looks different, huh?" said Misty.

Not only was the wall gone, the floors had been replaced with tile that covered the hardwood underneath. The walls were painted a dull gray that somehow made the whole section look brand new. "It's lovely. You did this?"

"All myself. Like, *really* myself. I did all the work."

"You removed that wall?"

Misty held up her fists. "You're not the only one who can use tools. Mine was the sledgehammer. Sledgehammer Misty."

"That's good," said Penny, smiling. "I'd go with Misty Sledge, though, if it were me."

"That does sound better. Anyway, there's my obsession." She pointed.

A huge TV was mounted on the wall. Underneath was a stand that held a speaker system. To the right was a bookcase filled with movies. Even from over here, Penny recognized her own titles. They were lined up on their own long shelf. On the other side was a theatrical poster of *Machete Mama*, the first movie of the series. It was slightly faded, which meant it was probably authentic and had come from an old movie theater somewhere in the world.

Penny's signature was scrawled across the bottom in purple marker. "Huh?" She looked at Misty, who looked like a bashful kid showing somebody her Barbie collection. "Where'd you get that?"

"eBay. Wasn't easy. Shipped from Hong Kong. Took a long time to show up."

"I remember signing them for the premier. They handed them out."

Misty nodded. "I got it from a son or grandson of one of the line producers. Or something like that. He has more stored away somewhere of other movies you did. But this one was my favorite. I really enjoyed it."

Penny faced the poster again, her eyes lingering on the title. *Machete Mama.* It was in a red font that filled the upper left corner of the poster in gritty flamboyance.

I was so young then. So in love.

Her life with Alex, their life together, had only just started. They'd had plans, lots of plans.

We barely got started before he was taken from me. Taken from us.

"Is it weird?" asked Misty.

Penny blinked, coming back from her memories. "What?"

"Is it weird that I have your poster on my wall?"

"No. Not at all. I uh...honestly, I thought you hated me."

"Hated *you?*"

Nodding, Penny turned her back on the poster. "You wouldn't tell me bye when I left."

A grimness washed over Misty's face. "I was mad that you were leaving. But I never hated you. I just didn't want you to go. You were the only friend I had. We'd been through everything together. I've always regretted not saying bye."

"You could've come with me."

"And did what? Hang out while you made kung-fu pictures? What would I have done out there, really?"

"You could've done it with me. Machete Mama and Sister Sledgehammer."

"What? I thought it was Misty Sledge."

"Sounds better."

Misty smiled. Her eyes began to shimmer. "It *does* sound better." She shrugged. "My place is here. If I'd left, I would've had to come back and take care of Mom after Dad died."

Penny stepped forward and put her arms around Misty. It hurt to do so, tugged at her stitches and the medical tape on her skin, but she didn't care.

At first, Misty acted as if she were hesitant to hug her back. After a few seconds, she raised her arms and put them delicately around her, careful not to hurt her.

They hugged for a while, and it felt good.

Misty pulled away first. There were wet trails leading down from the corners of her eyes. She laughed. "Wow. Look at us."

Penny knuckled her own tears away. "Couple of crybabies."

"I'll warm up the soup."

"Can't wait."

"Have a seat on the couch. I'll get the TV trays. We can eat like old people and watch TV."

Nodding, Penny made her way over to the couch and dropped down on it. The cushions felt like a cloud holding her. Though she hadn't been on her feet for very long, she felt exhausted and was glad to be sitting.

She hadn't eaten a meal in four days. She was almost trembling with anticipation for food. Was Anna being fed, wherever she was? Thinking about Anna brought her mind to Ashley.

In the deep freezer.

Like frozen meat.

Penny went tight inside. Her aching spots screamed. She couldn't believe her oldest daughter was in a freezer. Dead.

No. She's with Alex. She's happy.

But Penny was not. And Anna was probably in Hell.

Don't worry, baby. Mama's coming.

16

Penny had planned to leave Misty behind while she ditched the truck. Misty had argued with her that it was a job for two people, and she couldn't do it alone. As much as Penny wanted to prove she wouldn't need her help, she couldn't. Penny would have to drive the truck far out, leave it somewhere, and then hike to Aunt Kathy's cabin. After she fetched what she'd gone there for, she'd have to hike several miles back to Misty's house.

Her old friend was right. It would take two people to do it. Misty would have to follow her out there and drive her back when she was finished.

"I just don't want you to get hurt," said Penny. "Not you, too."

Misty smiled. She held up the mallet-sized sledge. "I'm bringing a weapon."

Penny had to admit that Misty did look pretty intimidating in her tight black jeans, matching tank top, and dark flannel. It made her hair stand out, the yellow-hued waves flowing down over her shoulders. Misty seemed to be in pretty good shape, with way more muscle than Penny had first thought.

She'd loaned Penny some fresh clothes as well. Baggy sweats and a loose T-shirt. The clothing was comfortable and clean.

Now Penny led Misty along the gravel roads that cut through the mountain. When they were younger, they used to take these roads whenever they snuck out of their houses for some joyriding. Sometimes those joyrides took place when neither of them was old enough to have a license. As often as they did it, they never got caught during any of their nighttime adventures.

Up ahead, Penny saw a turnoff section that stretched out from the main strip. She eased the truck over and shut it off. Misty waited for Penny on the road, her headlights off. Penny climbed out, looked around, and hurried over to Misty's SUV as fast as she could. Which wasn't very fast. Each step she took sent a burst of hurt through her body.

But she had to admit, the pain was fading. It was still there, but she felt better than she had this morning when she first woke up. And her belly was full. Hard not to feel slightly okay after eating two bowls of Misty's vegetable soup.

She quietly pulled the passenger door shut and leaned back in the seat. "Let's go."

Misty kept the headlights off as she drove. The moonlight cutting through the trees, sprinkling the road with silver flakes, provided enough radiance for them to see. "Are you sure we have to go by your aunt's cabin?"

"There's something I have to get."

"That's a bad idea."

"I know."

"They're probably watching her cabin in case you come back."

"I know that as well."

"Then why are you?"

"I told you. I need to get something."

Misty bit down on her bottom lip. Penny could tell there was more she wanted to say, but she kept whatever it was to herself.

They traveled to Aunt Kathy's property in obscure silence. Penny scanned the woods through the window. She saw no sign that anyone was out there, only foggy trees and lots of darkness. The frogs and crickets were so loud, she could hear them over the SUV's engine.

This is probably as good a place as any.

"Pull off here." Misty eased the compact vehicle onto the road's grassy edge. They were on the backside of the property. She'd have to trek through the woods the rest of the way.

"Why this spot?"

"I don't want them seeing *you*. I'll go the rest of the way alone."

"You're not ready for that kind of walk yet."

"I'll have to be."

Again, Misty nibbled on her lip. "I'll help you and—"

"No. I'll be fine. You stay here. Anybody comes along, get your ass out of here. Don't try to be a hero."

"Me?" Misty chuckled. It sounded forced. "I'm scared out of my mind."

"Keep the doors locked. Remember, you can't trust anybody from the sheriff's department. I don't know how far the corruption goes."

"I'm sure it goes all the way around."

"Remember…"

"I know. Haul ass if I see anybody."

Penny opened the door. The dome light came on, filling the cab with bright light. Misty covered the bulb with her hand, taking away the brightness. Penny pushed the door shut, bumping it with her hip. Even something as simple as that caused her aches to throb. Walking through the woods was going to be a brutal task.

And it was.

She had to stop and rest more times than she would have liked. But resting helped her. Whenever she pushed herself too hard, her body told her. A couple of times, everything went dizzy and splotchy. She leaned against a tree, closed her eyes, and breathed. She found those clouds, the warmth the golden aura brought, and let it all flow through her. It helped the dizziness to go away, helped her aches and pains to ease up. They didn't go away completely, but they were bearable. And that was all she needed for now.

Finally, she reached the end of the woods. Standing behind a tree, she scanned the backyard. The cabin was further out, a pale shape under the net of moonlight. Darkness piled down from the roof, surrounding the structure in black drifts. The windows were shadowy blocks. She saw nobody moving around, saw nobody standing guard. Maybe there wasn't anyone out there.

That doesn't make sense.

If they knew she was alive, which she figured they probably did, there would be eyes on this place. Even if she couldn't see them, they were there somewhere.

Penny scanned the yard again, then moved her focus to the woodshed. Her uncle had been a carpenter, using the shed as his workshop. He built everything from rocking chairs to footstools out there. When Penny was little, she used to love watching him work. She loved the sweet smell of cut wood, loved grabbing handfuls of sawdust.

In there was where she needed to go.

Penny stepped out of the woods. Standing at the launch of the yard, she scanned the area another time. Still no sign of anybody. She started moving. Every few steps, she looked around. She kept expecting to feel the kick of a bullet pounding her in the back.

Nothing happened.

She reached the back of the shed. There, she rested again, catching her breath. The oversized clothes clung to the sweat on her body, heavy and uncomfortable. If she could strip out of them, she would. It'd feel wonderful to have the night air on her skin, drying the sweat.

Not much more to do. Get it over with.

Penny let out another huff, then moved around the far side of the shed. Keeping her back to the wall, she studied the trees. She listened out for any sounds—a twig snapping, a scuttle, even an acorn dropping. She heard nothing, but the trilling sounds of the crickets.

She came to the corner, peeked her head around. Nobody stood there, either. Her uncle had replaced the shed's entrance with a rolling door that could be locked. It stood halfway open now, the inside of the shed stuffed with darkness. She had no idea if it had been open before because she hadn't had the chance to come out here when she and the girls had first arrived.

Most likely, it was. He'd died several years before, Aunt Kathy, and his grieving wife never came out here anymore.

Lady Striker killed Aunt Kathy, too.

There was no love lost there, but Penny still felt rage inside. All this had happened just to get Penny to come back here. Well, here she was. And now it was time to finish it for good.

Penny walked over to the shed, pulled the door open the rest of the way, and stepped inside.

Then she felt a burst of pain at the back of her head. Everything went white in a blinding glare that shut down her mind. As the buzzing starkness started to fade, Penny noticed she was on the ground on her knees. The leftover sawdust was soft and flaky underneath her. One hand was buried in it. The other held the back of her head where the throbbing jolts remained.

What had happened? She'd come into the shed and…what?

There were crunchy sounds of feet moving through the sawdust.

Somebody was in here with her.

Damn it!

She'd walked right into a trap.

"Sheriff said you'd probably come back. I didn't believe it."

She knew that voice. Trent? Wasn't that his name?

She risked opening her eyes, though it felt that if she did, her brain might squeeze through one of her eye sockets. The darkness was still there, but she could see the silhouette of the deputy standing over her. His badge gleamed dully. He was in his uniform.

Something clanked, a chain rattling.

Handcuffs.

Trent laughed. "I'm going to be so popular with Lady Striker. I caught the Machete Mother or whatever the hell they call you. She's gonna reward me. Oh, you wouldn't believe how good her rewards are. She's flexible, you know, from all that kung-fu shit. And it's unlike anything ever.

Crazy how stretching out a leg can make something feel like heaven."

"Asshole…" The insult fell off her tongue, slurred and heavy.

Laughing, he moved behind her, the darker shape of him shifting against the dark behind him. "Too bad I never got a piece of you. Tommy said your ass was tight as a fist. Maybe later. Maybe Lady Striker will let me before she kills you." The handcuffs rattled in her ear as they moved low, heading to her wrist. Penny waited for him to grab her. When he did, she jerked her arm. He let out a startled gasp as he fell toward her. She threw her other arm upward, connecting the ball of her hand with his chin.

Grunting, he fell onto the old sawdust with a sound like rustling leaves. He didn't stay there long. By the time Penny was getting to her feet, he'd already stood up and brandished his nightstick. He spun it around his hand. "You're gonna regret that, bitch."

Penny already did. She'd been aiming blindly at his forehead, hoping to put him out with one hit. But she couldn't see, so she'd missed and hit him too low.

"You're not the only one that knows how to kick ass. Lady Striker's shown us all a move or two."

His kick surprised her. She could smell his polished boot right before it bashed her cheek. She was back on the ground, on her side. She heard the nightstick whip through the air. Felt it coming toward her. She rolled out of the way. The dirt exploded behind her from the hit that barely missed her.

She springboarded to her feet. Swaying, she turned, dodging a triple attack of nightstick and fist combos. She twirled to avoid another kick. Hopefully, he'd tire himself out from the overly aggressive offense. He was coming at her in full force, too much and too fast. He wouldn't be able to keep it up. If she could keep avoiding them, she'd be okay.

He kicked her in the side. It wasn't a powerful kick, but he managed to hit her in a bad spot. Pain detonated through her midriff. On her way down, she brought up her arm, blocking another hit. He came back again, swung down. Getting to her knees, she brought her arm up to block again.

This time, it was the nightstick and not his boot.

The weapon knocked her arm out of the way. More pain raged through her. Her hurt arm dangled uselessly beside her. She tried to lift it. Couldn't. It was throbbing and dead.

"This has been fun," he said, "but it's time to wrap it up. I'd love to bash your skull in, but Lady Striker would have my ass if I did. She really hates you, you know. She insists that she's the one that has to kill you. But I can still hurt you as much as I want."

He was already swinging the nightstick again. Penny brought up her other arm to block the blow. She wasn't fast enough. The nightstick swiped over her knuckles on its path toward her face.

Just as she started to feel the slick tip of polished wood against her jaw, the nightstick broke in half. One piece twirled past her, fluffing her hair.

"The hell?" Trent said.

Penny looked up. The sledgehammer had intercepted the attack. Misty pulled it back, dropping the blunt end in her palm with a dull smacking sound.

Trent laughed. "What the hell is this? Misty? What're you doing here?" He looked down at Penny, then back at the other woman. "You're helping her?"

"Leave her alone," said Misty, squeezing the sledgehammer.

He drew his gun, training the barrel on her chest. "I'm only gonna tell you once, and that's because I used to go to your daycare. Get out of here."

What the hell is she doing? She's going to get herself killed!

"You always were a troublemaker, Trent. I knew you'd turn out this way."

"What way?"

"A shit." Misty ducked sideways, swinging up with the sledgehammer. It bashed Trent's elbow, snapped his arm, and knocked it upward with an awful cracking sound. Trent's howls of pain were even worse. His arm flopped and swung, the bones grinding.

"You fucked up my arm!"

Trent ran at Misty. As he reached her, he broke into a fighting stance. He threw chops with his good arm that she easily dodged. He did two roundhouse kicks, missing her both times. As he started to attempt a third, Misty slid through his stance, bringing up her knee as she leapt. His nose shattered under her kneecap. She flipped over his head, using his back for support as she came back and landed on both feet. The whole act looked mostly smooth and flawless.

She's been training.

Trent held his nose with the hand of his unbroken arm while the other dangled. He was no longer focused on Misty, so he didn't notice she was preparing to bash the back of his skull with the sledgehammer.

"Wait!" Penny said. Misty stopped the swing just before the heavy head was kissing the back of Trent's head. "We need him alive. For now."

"Does he need to be awake?"

"Not at the moment."

Lowering the sledgehammer, she shot out with her forearm. It caught the nape of his neck. Trent loosed another grunt, then dropped onto the sawdust in a limp heap.

"Cuff him," said Penny.

Misty searched the sawdust for the handcuffs. Finding them, she pulled his arms behind his back. His broken arm made grating sounds as she cuffed his wrists.

Misty turned to Penny. Even in the dark, Penny could see her bashful grin.

"You've been busy," said Penny.

"I've learned some stuff."

"How?"

"Studying your movies. I don't know a lot. But…"

"How long have you been doing it?"

"A couple years. I haven't been training like you did. Just what I have access to."

"Why? Because of my movies? Because you're a fan?" Penny's voice was rising. She took a deep breath, slowly letting it out. "You're lucky he didn't kill you."

"I'm lucky? You're lucky I came to check on you. You're lucky I helped you at all. I could've been a selfish bitch and thrown you out on your ass. What would you have done then?"

Penny lowered her head. Why was she so mad at Misty? *Because she could've been killed.*

"I've lost Alex and Ashley. Maybe Anna. I can't lose anymore…"

"I didn't learn the little bit that I know *because* of you. Well, not the way you think. I was…I was raped by an old boyfriend and his drunk friends. I'd never felt so helpless in all my life. Of course, Sheriff Charlie didn't do anything about it when I reported it because they were customers of his. I went home and watched your movie, *Private Justice*. The one where you trained the girl that was assaulted so she could get her revenge, the same way you'd gotten yours many years before in *Machete Justice*. So, I started training along with the characters. Just like you said in the movie, finding that outlet; it cleanses your soul. It releases you from a prison their actions put you in."

"Alex taught me that. I put it in the script."

"And you taught it to me."

"So, what do you plan to do with what you've learned?"

"I'm gonna go after them one day."

Penny nodded. She'd figured as much. She had no idea that any of this had happened. How could she have known? She'd been gone. She'd left Misty here alone with her parents. They'd passed away and left her completely alone.

"I'm sorry," said Penny.

"Yeah, well. I am, too. And they'll be sorry one day." Misty looked down at Trent. "Why are we here? I feel like all this could've been avoided."

"Help me up."

Misty came over and pulled Penny to her feet. She stifled a groan the pain tried to make her utter.

"Your arm is swelling."

Penny nodded. "Nothing's broken."

"You're sure?"

Another nod. "I'd know."

"Right. I guess you would."

Hobbling over to her uncle's workbench, she got down on a knee and opened the cabinet door. Inside was empty, save the wooden walls and floor of the cubby.

"What are you looking for?" asked Misty.

"Something I left here years ago, after I fought Lady Striker."

The wood was detachable, so she disconnected the floor section and slid it out. The dirt ground was underneath, dark and untouched for years. "There should be trowels hanging on the wall over there."

"I see them."

"Can you bring me one?"

Misty did. Penny stabbed the ground with the blade, flicking her wrist to toss heaping clumps of soil aside. She dug down a couple feet until striking something solid.

There you are.

Penny felt a nervous flutter inside. It'd been so long since she'd been so close.

Tossing the trowel over her shoulder, she gripped the cloth and pulled. It was hard to tug it from the ground with only one hand.

"What is it?" asked Misty.

The bundle clattered as Penny lowered it to the ground. "When I thought I'd killed Lady Striker the first time, I snuck out here. It was part of my plan. It was part of why I set it up for our fight to happen out here. I'd always have a place for them. I couldn't keep them in case the police came looking. And I didn't want to get rid of them forever. Alex made them for me, so after I threw Vanessa—Lady Striker off the mountain, I buried them here."

Dirt clung to the cloth, sprinkling away as she unwrapped. Though they'd been submerged in the earth for years, they still glinted in the darkness when she unveiled them. Seeing them again after so long filled Penny with another kind of warmth that she hadn't felt in forever.

Flexing her fingers, Penny grabbed a hilt with each hand and held them up.

Misty nodded. "That's really them? The same ones?"

"Yes. Sharpened to kill." Penny stood up, bringing her machetes with her. She held them out, a blade pointing away from her in either direction. It felt good to have them in her hands again.

It felt right.

She no longer felt so weak and feeble.

Her machetes were where they belonged—in her hands.

Penny slid the machete blade across her uncle's sharpening stone. Sparks fluttered as the workshop filled with the scraping sounds of grinding steel.

"Is that supposed to scare me?" asked Trent, laughing. He woke up a while ago. Now he sat on his knees in the sawdust piles, hands cuffed behind him. He winced each time he moved.

"Misty?" said Penny.

"Yeah."

"Go wait in the car."

"Hey. You can't…"

"I don't want you to see what I do next." Penny turned around. "It might change your opinion of me."

"I seriously doubt it."

"Do it. Please."

Trent laughed again, then hissed in pain.

Misty nodded. Her mouth was a tight line. She turned away and walked out of the workshop.

"Alone again," said Trent. "Just so you know, if you're thinking about torturing me for information or something, I get off on pain and bondage. It's my kink. I'm kind of a freak."

Penny walked over to him and ran the edge of a machete down his cheek. Blood flowed from the slit.

At first, Trent only flinched. But as the blood slid down to his jawline, he screamed. "You bitch! You messed up my face!"

Penny used the other machete on his other cheek, giving him a matching set. Now Trent was really screaming. He started to stand up, but Penny slammed a machete blade into the meaty part of his thigh. She pulled it free, flinging blood. The gash between the ripped section of his leg oozed blood onto his tanned pants. He dropped back down, groaning.

"You try to get up again, I'll cut off your foot."

"Fuck you!"

Penny stuck out her arm, putting the very tip of the machete against his bottom lip. "You like pain? I like putting people in pain. Maybe we're a match made in Heaven."

Trent's eyes nearly crossed as he stared down at the blade. "All right," he said. "You're fucking serious. All right."

Penny moved the machete away from his face. The tip left a little dot of blood behind. She returned to the workbench, bending and extending her hurt arm. Though it felt like rice was flowing under her skin, she was able to use it again. There'd be a nasty bruise to go with all the others, but she could live with that.

She sharpened the blades a bit more. It was easier to focus without Trent's constant remarks. Uncle Beau's chisel was in a drawer on his workbench. She pulled a machete close to her, hunched over the table, and placed the tip against the steel. She started to carve.

Ashley.

She blew away the grits clinging to the letters. Her oldest daughter's name stood out on the slick surface in a jagged scrawl.

Pulling the other machete to her, she repeated the process on the blade until *Anna* had been engraved on its side.

She held one in each hand. Her daughters' names were on the inner side of the blades, facing her. She could see each one.

"My girls," she said.

Trent's eyebrows lifted. "The fuck?"

"We're together again. It's always been you."

A machete for each daughter, one on each side, surrounding her even when she hadn't realized it. Had that been Alex's intention all along? His way of keeping the girls close to her even when they weren't.

Penny raised the blades. Then she kissed each one as she would her daughters' heads at bedtime when they were little.

"Oh, shit..." muttered Trent. He looked around. "Fuck."

He flinched when he saw Penny was focused on him again.

"How much are you going to make me put you through?" she asked.

Trent gulped. "Wh-what do you mean?"

She stepped closer, kicking sawdust out of her way. "You like pain?"

"I don't really...no. I don't like it that much."

"You said you do. You put my babies through a lot of pain."

"I was just doing what I was told. And I didn't really hurt anybody."

"Why didn't you get to hurt anybody? Do they not trust you?"

"I'm still new. I have to earn…" He stopped talking. "Shit."

"You have to earn what?"

"I don't wanna say."

"You better say." Anna was lowered to his crotch. "Nice and sharp."

"Fuck." He clamped his teeth together, huffing through his nose. "I have to work my way up. Like that night with you was Tommy's first time."

"I see. You're a rookie."

He nodded. "So, I didn't really hurt anybody. I just…stood in the hallway while Charlie, Tommy, and Eric had all the fun. I mean…*shit*. Not fun. While they…" He was almost crying as he tried to find his words.

"You were there. You were a part of it. You hurt them, you hurt me, just as much as the others."

"That's not true. I just…"

"You're a cop. You understand how the law works. Guilt by association. Right?" Trent closed his mouth again. He looked down. "See? You understand how it works. And this is my law now. My judgement. My sentencing. And my execution."

He shook his head. "If you wanted to kill me, you would have already. Right? That must mean that I have something you want. Whatever it is, I'll give it to you."

"You could've been a good cop," she said. "What I want is information."

"Name it."

"Where is Lady Striker?"

"I don't know."

"You were doing so well."

She jabbed Ashley into his side. Not very deep, but it still hurt him. He cried out. When she pulled the blade out, he emitted another cry. "Fuck! Why'd you do that?"

"Don't lie to me."

"I swear..." He was panting now. Tears made his face glossy. "They don't—"

Penny cut him off by stepping forward. She used Ashley to slice the side of his face again. While he screamed, she wiggled the tip of the blade behind the flap of skin. Through his flesh, she could see the shape of Ashley, lifting the skin, plucking it loose from the sinewy layer beneath. The skin peeled away from under his eye, flapping like thin latex. She knew where to cut, how to remove it the same way a special FX artist would remove a facial appliance.

"Stop! For fuck's sake, stop!" Trent bucked, falling sideways onto the sawdust. Ashley ripped through his skin, tearing half his face loose from below his eye. On his side, Trent screamed. He tried to raise his arms to hold the hurt spot, but they were cuffed behind his back. The movements seemed to aggravate his broken arm, which caused him to scream more.

The right side of his face dangled down to his cheek, exposing the stringy structure underneath. His eye was big and round, flicking this way and that.

"I don't know where she is! None of us do! Only Charlie!"

Penny knew going to the sheriff's station was way too dangerous, even for her. "Where can I find Charlie when he's conducting his *other* business?"

"The old hunter's lodge on Panther Peak. He owns it. That's where...that's where he does...everything."

"Is that where my daughter is?"

"That's where *all* the girls are..."

"All the girls?"

"Your daughter ain't the only one they've taken. People come from all over to get with young girls. They're always there, always paying."

"They'll die, too."

Trent gulped. "Are you done with me now? Please? I need medical attention."

"Get back on your knees."

"I can't..."

"Do it, or I'll pull the rest of you face off."

It wasn't easy for him, but he struggled back to his knees. He was slouched over, head hanging. The flap of skin hung from his face like a slice of bloody ham. "There. I'm up. Please... Are you done?"

"I'm done."

"Thank God. Thank God...please...let me go to..."

He stopped talking when Penny put both girls at his neck, crossing the blades into an X. "I'll let you go to Hell."

"Wait!"

She swiped both arms to opposite sides as if operating garden shears. Ashley and Anna sliced through his neck on either side, scraping together as they passed through. She brought her arms down as Trent's head shot upward, spinning. A trail of blood followed the angular section of his neck. His neck stump spurted blood. It coated the ceiling in crimson lattice patterns.

His head bounced over the sawdust, coming to a rest with his shocked face pointing at her. She kicked the side of his head. It bounced along the ground, rolled under the workbench, and dropped into the hole the machetes had been buried in.

She twirled, bringing both machetes down in a quick strike. The girls whacked Trent's chest and threw him to the ground.

Panting, Penny raised her girls and stared at their bloody blades. "One down, girls."

Penny left the work shed. Outside, the night was starting to fade as morning light seeped through the darkness.

They needed to get away from here.

18

The hot spray pounded her scalp, feeling wonderful as water sluiced down her naked back, sliding between her buttocks, and down her legs. Penny stood under the showerhead with her eyes closed. Her hair was plastered to her face and shoulders.

She'd washed herself twice with Misty's soap. She was shiny and slick and clean. She wasn't sure she'd ever taken a shower that had felt this wonderful.

Turning, she put the back of her head against the spray. If this were a movie, the director of photography would have pulled back the camera to make sure the lens captured a good shot of her large breasts.

"Other than the fighting," a producer would say, "it's what the audience loves to see!"

She hadn't always done nude scenes in her films, but sometimes she felt it was okay. If the story wasn't dependent on her showing T and A, and it could be handled in a tasteful way, she would do it. Naturally, those movies were the ones that always made more money.

Yeah? What about Machete Mutilator? It tanked, and you did a whole fight scene completely naked.

Machete Mama had been attacked while using one of those outdoor shower systems at a camp. She was naked in the shower. She had to fight for her life without any clothes on. She wouldn't pause to get dressed if her life was in danger. Of course not.

At least, that was how the director had pitched it to her.

"Plus," he'd said, "showing all your skin will help us sell to Italy at a higher price. They love your tits out there!"

Penny looked down at her naked torso and frowned. Wouldn't any camera want to film the stitches and bruises, the welts and scrapes under the bandages now. She was in bad shape, a science experiment that had gone horribly wrong.

Maybe Frankenstein would enjoy it.

She almost smiled at that thought. *Machete Frankenstein.* They'd missed a chance at that one.

Out of nowhere, Penny started to sob. She turned around, pushing her face into the heavy spray. It washed away the tears as soon as they came. Her shoulders shook as the weeping poured out of her. Hugging herself, she nestled into the corner of the shower, enjoying the coolness of the tile wall. Pressing her face against it, she sighed. The tears abated.

Where'd that come from?

Sniffling, she took several deep breaths.

She'd killed another person tonight. That was two dead by her hand, and she felt nothing.

They deserved it.

Did they? Does anybody deserve what she'd done to them?

Yes.

She wasn't crying because of Levi, Trent, or how violently she'd killed either. She was crying because of Anna. Her youngest daughter was still out there, in danger. Probably had given up, probably had zero hope at all that she would ever get out of the awful dilemma she was in.

I'm coming, baby.

At least she knew where to find them.

And Charlie can lead me to Lady Striker.

There was a knock at the door. Misty's muffled voice said, "You okay?"

Penny stepped back from the wall. She sniffed. Though the shower sprayed her face, she still wiped it with the back of her hand, as if trying to hide her tears. "Yeah! I'm okay."

"You sure? It sounded like you were crying."

I was.

"I'm okay. Thanks for checking on me."

There was a pause before Misty said, "Of course. Holler if you need me."

"I will."

Penny stood there, giving Misty time to go back into the living room. She stuck her face in the spray again, opening her mouth and filling it with hot water. She spit it out, then dropped her head, letting the pelting pressure massage the back of her skull.

I need to get out and dry off. Put on fresh bandages. Sleep.

She didn't want to move. The water was perfect. But she knew if she didn't get out soon, Misty would probably come back and check on her again.

Penny shut off the water. Standing there, she listened to the water drops fall from the nozzle. More drizzled off her body, tapping the bottom of the tub. To her surprise, she wasn't as sore as she should've been. Even the back of her head, where Trent had bashed her with his club, hardly hurt at all.

But that was how it used to be, back when she filmed regularly and trained with Alex. He taught her how to overcome her aches, how to not only work against her limitations, but to excel with them.

How to heal.

It was almost supernatural. She said the same thing to Alex once. He'd given her that smile that usually made her forget where she was for a few seconds.

"It's not supernatural," he said. "It's archaic. And it chooses who gets to know about its power."

"What power?" She'd felt tingly inside, as she usually did whenever he talked about the ancient ones.

"*Their* power." He pointed to the flags that had hung in his dojo, where he'd trained her and several members of his crew. But no one had been taught everything like Penny.

The flags were old. She never asked how old they were, but she assumed they'd been crafted centuries ago.

"It's like magic," he said. He put his hand flat on her chest above her right breast. "And it's in your heart."

A corner of Penny's mouth lifted. "You just wanted to touch my tit."

Alex laughed. "I always want to do that. But this time, it wasn't *all* I was trying to do."

Penny stepped over to him. He put his arms around her, pulling her tightly against him. They kissed.

Standing in the shower stall now, Penny could almost feel his lips against hers. But he wasn't there. She was alone.

And naked.

Penny took a deep breath, stretching out her lungs. After the crying spell, they felt tight. She expected to feel that familiar sharp poke from her broken ribs. But other than a dull soreness, she felt nothing. Putting her fingers in the ridges of her ribcage, she ran the tips up and down her wet skin.

They're not broken anymore.

Alex's magic had worked again.

It's not magic.

That had been Alex's voice.

"It's ancient," she muttered to herself.

Pulling back the shower curtain, she stepped over the tub and onto the bathmat. A fresh towel hung from the brass ring attached to the wall. She used it to dry herself, then used the bandages Misty had given her to redress the wounds. Another day or two, she might not need to cover them at all.

Her forearm had started to heal as well, but there was still a dark circle on each side. She wrapped it, spinning the gauze in layers. When she was finished, she put on the nightshirt. Like everything else, it was a loaner from Misty. And since her friend was taller, the long shirt hung down past her knees. She felt like a gnome as she walked over to the foggy mirror.

She wiped a clear path on the glass, revealing her face—pale, wet hair in tangles, a split lip and fading scratches on her cheeks. The black around her eyes was waning, though the left was still red from busted blood vessels. Neither looked very puffy anymore.

She used Misty's hairbrush on her hair. She took her time, making delicate strokes as she worked through the knots. At times, the brush became jammed in her hair, and she had to work to get it loose. When her hair was finally smooth, and she could run her fingers through it, her scalp was tingling. It was amazing how something as simple as brushing your hair could help you feel better.

A brand-new toothbrush, still in the packaging, was on the counter. A travel-sized tube of toothpaste was beside it.

Smiling, Penny opened the toothbrush.

Misty's always prepared.

When she was done in there, she stepped into the hall. From the steamy warmth of the bathroom, the cool air felt wonderful. She sighed.

From the living room, Misty grunted.

Shit!

Penny spun on her heels and ran up the hall. Misty gasped from around the corner, then gave another grunt. Sounded like she was in a struggle.

Penny dashed into the room, ready to fight.

Misty, dressed in athletic shorts and a halter top, whipped around. On one foot, her other leg was fully extended. Her toes were arched, as if she were about to execute a perfect kick. She spotted Penny and yelled in fright, which caused Penny to yell back, startled by Misty's reaction.

"What the hell, Penny?" she yelled, lowering her leg.

"*Me?* What the hell are you doing?" She looked over at the TV. She saw herself on the screen, fighting two goons in a restaurant. *Machete Mercenaries,* a later entry in the franchise, where Machete Mama had to assemble a special team of badasses to bring down a warlord from another dimension.

Misty, face flushing from either exertion or embarrassment, grabbed the remote control and paused the movie. She tossed it on the couch. She stood, hands on her hips, huffing. "You scared the shit out of me!"

"Sorry. But *you* scared me first. I heard you making...noises and thought..."

Misty looked at the TV, then back to Penny with an expression a kid might make after getting busted watching a porno. "I figure it's as good as being trained by you."

Penny saw the frozen image of her own face scrunched into an angry sneer as she was about to throw a series of punches into a masked man's stomach. She remembered how the filming of this picture had gone very well, with very little delays, only for the movie to be released and tank in almost every market. It did, however, find an audience in the video stores and on cable in America.

Turned out the fans only wanted to watch Machete Mama enact her own brand of justice. They weren't very interested in her leading a team of vigilantes. The change in the series' direction had been Penny's idea because she had become the mother of two children and wanted to spend less time on set and more time at home. Filming close to a dozen movies a year was starting to burn her out. And she just wanted to be a mom for a while and let other characters fill in for her while she was gone.

It didn't work out like that.

"Is this weird?" asked Misty.

Penny shook her head. "No. Well, not *too* weird."

Grimacing, Misty sank onto the couch. She stretched out her long legs. "I told you they helped me. The movies, I mean. Machete Mama helped me. I know that probably sounds weird. Makes me sound like a fanatic or something."

"There was a time when she helped me, too. When Alex and I created her, she changed our lives. For the better. But she also ruined another person's life, which led to everything getting destroyed."

"Just like you told me before—Lady Striker had already done that to herself before you even came along. You said…" She stopped talking when Penny waved her hand.

"Maybe she could've changed. Maybe she should've been given the chance to."

"Or maybe she'd had enough chances. Maybe there weren't any left to give her."

Most likely, Misty was right. But Penny would never be able to fully believe it. She'd created the real Lady Striker herself. And by doing so, she'd created the real Machete Mama.

It all sounded like the plot of one of her movies, a meta take on the material where life imitated art.

"I'll turn it off," said Misty. She grabbed the remote.

"No. It's fine."

"I think I've made things weird now. Worse than they already were."

"You didn't." Penny stared at the back door. Misty's dad's shop was right out there, where Misty had hidden the truck. When they'd gone to dump the truck earlier, she'd only glanced at the freezer.

Ashley.

Misty shut off the movie. "It's pretty late. Maybe we should get some sleep. I have some painkillers you can take. They were Mom's. They might not be as strong as they used to be, so you might want to take two."

Penny was already heading for the back door. She hadn't realized she was going to until she'd taken the first step.

"Penny?"

Penny looked back over her shoulder. Misty had come forward. Her bare stomach was shiny under the light from the table lamp. "What are you doing?"

What *was* she doing?

Penny suddenly felt ashamed, as if she'd been caught going through Misty's underwear drawer. "I...I'm not sure. I thought I might…"

"Don't go out there. She's there until you can properly give her a resting place. You don't need to see her…the way she is."

"I've seen her already." Though that was true, she had a hard time remembering her oldest daughter's condition. That was probably a good thing.

"Maybe so. But she's fine out there. Seeing her now won't help you in any way."

Penny gritted her teeth. She knew this already. But she still wanted to go out there. She'd always peeked her head in on the girls after they were asleep, just to check on them, to watch them sleep for a little while. She'd been excited to do it in the cabin the other night because both her daughters were under the same roof again.

And it was taken from me.

She'd never be able to peek in on both girls ever again. Maybe neither of them.

"Penny? Come back to the living room. Sit down. Let's just…I don't know. Hang out."

Penny sighed. She'd been exhausted after her shower and could've gone right to sleep. Now she felt restless. Trying to sleep now would be pointless. And she did *not* want to take any pain meds to help with that issue.

She wanted to hit something.

Penny looked at Misty. "How about you put that movie back on and we practice together?"

"Oh, Penny. You shouldn't be doing anything physical. Especially after…" She stopped talking. Probably because she realized Penny was ignoring her as she headed back to the living room.

Misty had slid the couch and coffee table back to make room for her exercises. "You want to learn, and I need to practice."

"But your stiches..." Misty stepped into the living room, looking nervous. "They might rip."

"I know my limitations."

Misty stared at her for another moment, then slowly started to smile. "Okay. That'll be neat, to train with you."

"Actually, do you have the first movie?"

"*Machete Mama?* The original?"

"Yeah. The training montage in that would be perfect to practice with. We can put the scene on repeat."

"Asking me if I have it? Please. I only have a framed poster of it hanging on the wall." Misty walked over to a bookcase. The top shelf was full of movies standing up with their spines facing out. She didn't even hunt for it. Her hand went straight to where it was.

Penny could see the cover from where she stood. It matched the poster Misty had tracked down on eBay. "Do you know where the scene is that I'm talking about?"

Misty, on the floor, had already removed *Machete Mercenaries* and was putting the other disc on the tray. "I can skip right to it. I know every scene by heart."

A minute or so later, Misty had the scene pulled up and paused. Standing, she held the remote control in her hand. "What do we do now?"

Penny walked over and stood beside her. "Well, you're warmed up, but I'm not. I need to stretch first."

"It's going to hurt."

"Probably so."

The stretches that normally felt so wonderful, felt like they might make her heart stop. More than once, she cried out, worrying Misty. After twenty minutes of excruciating physical activity, Penny was drenched in sweat. Her hair had only been mildly damp after her shower, but was soaked again.

"I need to check your stitches," said Misty.

Penny was on her back on the carpet, panting. She held up her hand. "They're fine."

"Pull the shirt up." Misty got on her knees beside her.

"You're going to see me in *your* skivvies."

"I've seen you naked in the movies. Plus, I sponge-washed you when you first got here."

"Damn. Hate I missed that."

"You should. I'm good at it." Misty smiled. "Shirt. Lift."

Sighing, Penny pulled the shirt up. She raised her rump off the floor and got it out from underneath her. She stopped when she reached her breasts. The cool air felt wonderful on her sweaty skin.

She felt Misty's fingers gently pushing her abdomen. "How is that possible?"

"What?"

"You're healing *very* fast."

"Ancient medicine."

Misty looked down at her. Strands of her hair had fallen out of the messy bun she'd tied on her head. "I'm going to pretend I know what you're talking about."

"I'll explain one day. I might be healing, but I'm still sore and weak. I need to train."

Nodding, Misty tugged the shirt down, covering Penny again. "I'll grab us some bottles of water. Then we can get started."

The first attempt to follow along with the montage was a disaster. Penny got behind many times while Misty prospered. There were moves her old friend was unable to perform, but she still fared better than Penny.

"Should we stop?" asked Misty, out of breath.

Penny gulped water, twisted the cap back on. "Nope. Start it over."

The second time went better, but Penny still couldn't keep up. It was as if she wasn't the one who'd choreographed the whole montage herself. This was a routine she'd constructed for the movie and had followed for many years until she'd changed it up and added more moves and combos.

"How're the stitches?" asked Misty when they'd finished a third round.

Penny reached up under the shirt and fingered the thread. She felt sweat, but no blood. "We're still good. Play it again."

They kept at it for another hour. Each time the montage reached its conclusion, Misty skipped it back to the beginning of the scene where Machete Mama enters the forest. She walks along the path that Wu, the sensei, had taken her on while explaining the healing factors of martial arts. Little had Penny known at the time how accurate and truthful his monologue had been.

"Your bones may break, but the spirit of the ancient warrior that resides in you will heal it. Your own spirit is also broken, but it is not dead. Your body is the vessel. The true warrior lies within. Heart, soul, and body will work as one."

Machete Mama finds the clearing in the movie and starts off the montage with a series of hits and chops.

"Okay, Misty," said Penny. "Make sure you have your thumb folded like this. Don't swing down, come up and in like this." She showed her.

Nodding, Misty did what she was told.

"Perfect. This time, come at me as you do it."

"What?"

"Don't hold back."

"Don't hurt me."

"*Try* to hurt me."

"Jesus."

"Come on!"

Misty repeated the move, chopping at Penny's face. She'd been a fool to worry that Misty might have held back. She came at her with everything she had, chopping and swinging with both arms. Penny ducked and weaved, brought up her arms and blocked them. With each attack, they moved back another step or two, stopping when Penny's back touched the wall.

"Good," said Penny. "We just did the opening part."

Misty huffed. "We did, didn't we?" She smiled, shook the hair out of her eyes. "That's what you were doing in the movie."

"But in the movie, there wasn't somebody to train off of, so I was pretending there was. Come on. Let's do the next part."

Penny was still a little slow, but she stayed in sync with Machete Mama on screen, much better this time. They paused the scene, then practiced with each other, going back and forth with kicks and chops. Penny managed to jump, flipping over Misty's back and landing where the coffee table usually sat. She wobbled slightly, quickly regained her composure, and resumed her fighting stance.

Misty, smiling, twirled around and threw out a kick. Penny dodged it, caught her by the ankle, and tickled the bottom of her bare foot.

"Stop!" Misty said, laughing.

Releasing her foot, Penny stepped forward. She was panting. Her hair was a mess, and her skin was shiny under a sweaty sheen. "I'm going to have to take another shower."

Misty took a deep breath and let it huff out. "You and me both."

"One more time," said Penny, "then we'll call it a night."

"A morning," said Misty, pointing at the window.

Penny looked and saw that night had passed into the early morning. Mist floated outside the glass, thinning as gilded light pushed away the shadows and began to shine. Penny looked back at Misty. "Then let's take this outside."

In the backyard, Penny and Misty stood facing each other. Penny took a deep breath, shoving away the apprehension and fear that continued to gnaw at her.

You can do this. You have many times before.

Not only could she do it. She created it.

"Ready!" Penny yelled. Her voice echoed through the trees. The morning air was light and cool on her skin.

Misty jerked into a fighting stance, just as Penny did. Their eyes locked. Penny nodded, then Misty attacked. If she'd been holding back even slightly inside, out here she was unleashed. Misty came at her, hard and fast, throwing chops and upper kicks.

Penny met each strike with a block and a grunt. Misty had backed her toward the deck. Penny stopped before reaching it and smiled. "My turn."

"Don't hold back. I have to learn."

"I won't. And don't take it personally."

"Huh?" Fear washed over Misty's face for a moment. It was replaced by a grinning scowl. "Bring it."

Penny attacked. "Kiai!" Each time she threw an offensive strike, the forceful exhale shot out of her mouth. She focused on each one, channeling her energy through her breaths. Misty managed to block a couple of strikes, but her defensive victories didn't last. By the time Penny finished her offense, Misty was on the ground.

On her back in the grass, Misty stared up at the sky, moaning. "Thank God you didn't hold back."

Penny stood on one foot, slightly tilted, with her other leg extended. Her toes were arched. The night shirt had slid back to show her whole leg. The bruises were faint markings on her skin now and no longer looked like tiger stripes.

Penny chopped through the air with her hands, folding them into fists and swinging this way and that. She rolled her arms, bringing them down, and pulled back to mimic the pose from the *Machete Mama* poster.

Misty watched her from the ground. "Outstanding."

Lowering her leg, she put her foot on the grass. She stepped over to Misty, offering her hand. "Breakfast?"

Smirking, Misty took the proffered hand. She gasped when Penny yanked her to her feet. "Whoa! Wasn't expecting that."

Laughing, Penny sighed. "I'm hungry. You got any bacon?"

"I've got the works, dear."

"Tag team breakfast? You do the bacon. I'll do the eggs?"

"Eggs are easier."

"Right. And you lost, so you get to do the bacon."

Misty smirked.

Penny held out her hands. "What if I do the toast too?"

"That's better."

"But you have to make the coffee."

"Deal."

They headed back inside.

20

Penny mopped up the rest of the yolk on her plate with her toast, then she tossed it in her mouth. She'd cleaned her plate, but somehow still felt hungry. Misty must have too because she sliced up a plate of strawberries, kiwi, and bananas and set it on the table.

Penny took a strawberry and kiwi from the plate. "I feel like a pig."

"You?" Misty stepped over to the table with the coffeepot. "I ate just as much as you did." She refilled their mugs, then returned the pot to the hot plate. She sat down and joined Penny in adding sugar and creamer.

Penny sipped her coffee. It was hot and good. She put the mug down and sighed. "Alex said he loved my appetite."

Misty drank some coffee. "What was he like?"

Penny saw Alex in her mind and felt every good emotion he'd ever caused all at once. Her skin warmed, tingled. Her heartbeat sped up. "He was everything. He taught me so much, taught me how to truly live. How to…have joy. True joy. True happiness."

"And he taught you to fight?"

"Everything I know, I learned from him."

"He trained Lady Striker too?"

"Yes. But he didn't teach her like he did me. Alex said it was during their lessons when he began to sense who she truly was. She used and abused what she learned, so Alex stopped teaching her and started teaching me. She didn't like that. Honestly, I wasn't sure how *I* felt about it. But I finally felt complete with Alex and martial arts. I was sort of, I don't know, *guided* into the role of Machete Mama. I was just a day player for several productions that was promoted to the role of the villain. But the producers and fans loved Machete Mama. And she took everything from Lady Striker."

"No. Lady Striker *lost* it all. Machete Mama was there to pick it up."

"Look at it through her eyes. And really, most people would sympathize with her if this were a new Lady Striker movie. Machete Mama would once again be the villain who took everything from the hero, including the life she *could've* had. Machete Mama went on to fame overseas and throughout the world thanks to the Hong Kong action movie boom in the nineties. She got married, had two amazing daughters, and the family life in the Hollywood Hills amongst other celebrities. Lady Striker's life."

Sipping coffee, Misty shook her head. "Lady Striker would never have wanted that. She'd want to be worshipped like a queen. You know this. And if you think about it, now she is. She's got everything she wanted. Men work for her. She rules over them. They idolize her. She is a celebrity among the shady side of the world now. The mysterious leader that nobody knows about unless they're about to be killed by her."

Penny lowered her head, thinking of Ashley.

Seeing this, Misty reached out a hand. "Sorry. I didn't mean it like that."

"It's okay," said Penny. "I know what you meant."

"But you shouldn't hate yourself because of the way things worked out for Lady Striker. You should hate her for what she's done to you and your family."

"Alex taught hate is never a virtue you should bring into a fight. It clouds your judgment; it drowns your emotions. You get sloppy. But right now, I'm not fighting. And you're right, I hate her. I hate her with every fiber of my body and my soul."

"Good," said Misty. "If you didn't hate her, I'd never be able to understand that."

"But when I face her again, I will shut off the hate. I'll shut off all my emotions. That's what happened to me the last time we met. My pity kept me from confirming her demise. I felt that she'd suffered enough and left her to die on her own. She didn't. And now Ashley is…gone. If I'd made sure, if I'd…"

"Penny."

Holding up her hand, Penny used her finger on her other hand to wipe the tears from her eyes. "I know. It's not wise to dwell on things of the past that can't be changed. But it's a fact, Misty. My decision, my clouded judgement, got my first born killed. I will *not* let anybody else I care about die because of my poor strength of will."

"Isn't that emotion clouding your mind again?" Misty grabbed Penny's hand across the table, holding it in hers. "We'll do this together."

Penny snatched her hand back. "No."

"Penny—"

"I said 'no', Misty. This is my fight. It's dangerous. And I'm not putting you in the middle of it anymore. I have enough already. If they find out you've been helping me, they'll kill you. Your participation ends now."

Misty leaned back in the chair. "You need my help. Two is better than one."

"I might need it, but I'm not taking it. You're my friend, Misty. I'm grateful for you. I always have been. I hate how I walked away from you when I left this place behind. But my life was meant to be away from here. That doesn't mean I should've cut all ties with you. I'm sorry for that."

"Penny..."

Penny kept talking. "But I'm not taking you with me."

"I'll just go, anyway. I can't let you go alone. You're going on a suicide mission. You can't face them all by yourself."

"No. But Machete Mama can."

"Jesus." Misty went to drink more coffee, then seemed to change her mind. She stood up and walked over to the sink. "How will you killing yourself help Anna at all?"

"If she's safe, it'll help her plenty." Penny stood up. "I'm ending this tonight, Misty. Once and for all."

Misty stared out the window above the sink. "You're not even healed all the way. You need me. I know I'm not as good as you. Not even close. But I'm pretty good. Better than most of them would be. Together, we'd be able to stop them."

Penny crossed the kitchen and stood beside her friend. "You're really not going to let me win this one. Are you?"

Misty looked over at her, a corner of her mouth rising. "I'm not."

"Jeez…" Penny shook her head. She stepped forward, holding her arms open.

Smiling, Misty stepped into the embrace and hugged her back. "I lost you once. I'm not losing you again."

Penny tightened her hug. "You won't. I hope you understand why I did this when you wake up."

Misty froze. "Huh?"

Penny reached up behind Misty, curving her arm over her shoulder. She quickly found the spot on her neck that Alex had taught her about. A pressure point, that if pinched just right, would render the person unconscious for a few hours. But the key of the trick was getting them when their defenses were down. They had to be totally at ease.

Penny found it just as Misty started to resist. When she pinched it, Misty went limp in her arms. She fell against Penny. Arms dangling, her head lolled on her shoulders.

"I'm sorry, Misty. But I can't risk anything happening to you."

Dragging Misty, she made her way up the hall and into Misty's room. She reached the bed and situated Misty on top, gently resting her head on a pillow. She left her friend in the athletic clothes she had on and stripped off the sodden nightshirt she'd been wearing. Going to Misty's dresser, she rummaged through the drawers and found a pair of jeans, a tank top, and a bra.

Hopefully, you don't mind I borrow these.

She'd replace them when she was done. After all, they were bound to get very bloody.

The jeans were ripped, leaving sections of her thighs showing. Penny had no idea if they'd been like this when Misty bought them, or if they'd just started to tear with age. Didn't matter. She was just glad they fit.

Penny found a pair of boots in the closet. Their aged appearance, she could tell, had come from time. They fit her a little snug, but that was okay. She'd rather them be that way than loose when she kicked. Didn't want one to fly off while she was fighting.

Stopping by the bathroom, she used the toilet, then brushed her hair. She pulled it back off her shoulders and tied it. She peeked in on Misty again and found her snoring on the bed.

Good.

On her way to the kitchen, she shut off the TV. The paused image of Penny in her fighting stance faded away. She took a couple bottles of water from the fridge, added them to a cinch bag she found in the pantry, hung it on her shoulders, then headed outside.

Her next stop was the shop outside. She stood in the doorway, staring at the freezer. Her throat tightened, thinking of Ashley inside. Misty's warning replayed in her mind. Her friend was right. She shouldn't see her in there like that, wrapped in thick plastic and frozen.

Especially when Ashley and Anna were already on the table to the left of her.

"Hey, girls." Penny spoke the same way she would have if they'd just come home from school. "I'm back." She walked over to the table and lifted the machete sheaths. She strapped them to her legs, then lifted Ashley from the table. She kissed the cold side of the blade before sliding her into the sheath. "All warm now." Picking up Anna, she kissed her also. "Mama's coming." Then she added her to the empty sheath on her other leg.

See, Misty? I'm not alone. The girls will be with me.

Here was the part that Penny had dreaded before, but now she wondered why. Penny Chambers got to go away for a while. And that was what was best. Penny Chambers would mess up, would somehow show compassion when it wasn't deserved. She'd get tired, weakened. So, she had to go.

Machete Mama needed to come out and handle things from here.

In her mind, a door opened, and the conscience of Penny Chambers floated out like a draft carried through a breeze. The essence of Machete Mama floated in, filling the void in her mind and hammering the doors and windows shut.

Penny Chambers wouldn't be allowed back in for a while.

Maybe not ever again.

Back outside, Machete Mama headed for the woods. It was going to be a long hike to the hunter's lodge. But she could handle it. The excursion would be good for her. She could also take breaks along the way, do exercises and train in preparation. She wasn't going to take Misty's car. If anybody recognized it, they'd go after Misty. Machete Mama wouldn't let that happen. A long walk to protect Penny's best friend would be worth it.

The trees provided plenty of welcome shade. She listened to the birds sing, the chirps that carried melodies all through the woods. It was lovely compensation for the bloodshed that was coming. The violence.

For the other part of Machete Mama's life, that brought her the same kind of joy Alex had brought to Penny Chambers.

Killing people that deserved it.

Anna's blade tore through the guard's back, throwing blood against the tree. He'd been standing off, alone, lighting a cigarette when Machete Mama approached him. She'd moved silently, her boots whispering across the pine needles strewn all over the forest floor.

Anna, in Machete Mama's right hand, shot out just as the man started to turn around. His eyes rounded when he spotted her. Then they screwed shut when the machete punched into him.

She let him drop. He slid off the blade.

"What was that, Arn?" Another man's voice came from the other side of the tree.

Machete Mama heard the crunches of his footsteps as he closed in. Sounded like he was coming in from the right. She slipped to the left, stepping around the side of the tree just as the new guy stepped around the other side.

"Shit! Arn!"

Machete Mama hurried around the backside of the tree, coming back around the same side he'd entered from. Now he was in front of her, shorter than the first guard. Like the other one, he also wore camouflage.

As he sank down to check on his comrade, Machete Mama stepped up behind him. She lowered Ashley, turning the sharp side inward and putting it in place. He noticed it too late and only managed to let out a surprised gasp before she slashed his throat open. Blood dumped onto Arn's dead body, dousing him in the other guy's life juice.

Straining to scream, the other man could only produce strangled breaths. A hand to his throat, he twisted sideways and saw her. His eyes grew wide before the life fled from them and took away the brown color.

He fell on top of Arn, dead as well.

With both men eliminated, she was able to check around the surrounding area. They seemed to be the only two in this section of woods. She hurried through the trees, stopping when she reached the edge of the ridge that rose above the clearing down below.

The hunter's lodge sat back behind a strip of trees, as if it were hiding. The sun was high near the distant peaks, washing the smokey layer of clouds in warm light. Nobody was walking around out there. She saw trucks parked in a clearing alongside Charlie's police-issued SUV.

It had taken Penny close to four hours to hike out here, yet she hardly felt any exhaustion. She was moving on instinct alone. Letting her spirit guide her body, opening it up to the ancient ones' direction.

Crouching behind a rock, Penny watched for a while. Only a few times did she see anybody move about. Nobody seemed to be on high alert. Of course not, she thought. They weren't expecting her to come after them during the day. She didn't doubt they'd discovered she'd killed Trent. They knew she was going to come after them. But they were

In her mind, Machete Mama stepped back and let Penny fully experience her reunion. She couldn't give her much time because at any moment now somebody would notice the people she'd killed.

Anna buried her face against Penny's chest, sobbing. She could feel the warm tears seeping through her tank top.

"I can't believe Ashley's gone. I wanna go home. They hurt me…They took turns…doing things to me…

"How's your arm?"

"Huh?" Anna glanced at the bandage. "Oh. They stitched it up, but they haven't touched it since."

Penny pulled back, lifting Anna's head with both hands. She looked into her daughter's eyes. "You need to get out of here. Head straight to the woods, find the path, and get moving. Follow it straight into the mountain."

"Mom."

"Listen. When you get to the stream, cross it."

"I can't, Mom. I—"

"You'll come to a spot where the paths intersect. Go straight until you reach the gravel road. It's a long walk, but you'll eventually come to a driveway. That's Misty's house. She's my friend. Go there. She'll protect you."

"I'm not leaving you, Mom." Anna shook her head. "I won't. You…" She seemed to see Penny for the first time. The grimace on her face was hard to hide. "My God…"

Penny looked down at herself. Blood was spattered all over her clothes in shiny splashes. She had crimson streaks on her arms as if she'd been swimming in jam. She looked up at Anna and tried to give her a comforting motherly smile. "They were all bad men."

Anna hugged herself, trembling. "There're others."

"I'll kill them, too."

Mama ran up to him, tugging Ashley free. She slashed his throat as she passed, leaving him gurgling.

Reaching the front, her head swiveled. Nobody was coming. She went to the door. It was bolted and had a massive lock for additional security.

She grabbed the handle on the plate covering the window and yanked it to the side. She pressed her face close to the barred rectangle. It was dark in there. The sunlight spilled in, cutting a bright block out of the shade inside. She could hear quiet sniffling.

"Anna?"

The sniffling stopped. "Mom?"

"Anna!"

"Oh…God…Mom!"

Though Machete Mama knew the door was locked, she still tried to open it. "I'm here, baby. I'm here."

"I knew you'd come for me. I…knew it…"

"Hang on. I have to get the keys."

She searched the dead guards, finding the keys on the first one she killed. Returning to the door, she unlocked it and flung it open. Light spilled in, shoving the darkness against the walls and exposing Anna on the dirt ground. Naked, her pale skin was striped with dark smudges. A dirty bandage covered the ax wound on her arm. Though it had only been a few days since she'd last seen her, she could tell her daughter had lost significant weight. She could see the dips of her ribcage and her cheekbones looked as if they were trying to tear through her face. Her wrists and ankles were in manacles attached to chains.

She found the key on the set and unlocked the thick bracelets. Now that she was free, Machete Mama pulled Anna close and wrapped her arms around her. Her skin somehow felt cold and sweaty at the same time.

She kept walking, wrenching the machete from his head on the way.

Faint voices came from inside the lodge. She thought she recognized Charlie's southern drawl. Her insides began to squirm. She could feel him inside her again, ramming and hurting her. She almost veered toward the lodge's back door, kicked it in, and entered whatever was waiting on the other side.

But that had to wait. She needed to check out the smaller building first. If Anna was in there, she needed to get her out.

Machete Mama ran across the grass, pressing herself against the lodge's wood siding. She could feel the splinters poking her through her tank top. Peeking around the edge, she saw the two guards hadn't moved. Both stood at either corner, facing opposite directions. Both guys were big.

Backtracking, she slipped back into the woods and started making her way around. As she approached the back of the shed, she put Ashley and Anna in their sheaths. Then she slid three of the smaller blades from her calf.

She scanned the area, saw nobody else wandering around, and rushed out of the trees. She stopped a few feet on the grass and whistled. Just as she expected, the big boys stepped out from their spots by the door.

A blade punched into the one on the right's throat. The other guy jumped out of the way as his buddy fell to the ground, twitching. He spotted Machete Mama, realized she must've been the one who'd thrown the knife, and started to raise the rifle.

Two other small knives punched into him, one imbedding into his chest and the other into his stomach. Dropping the rifle, he sank to his knees, groaning. Machete sputter as he collapsed, throwing a wet line across the bark of the tree in front of him.

She saw the knives he had in sheaths on his ankles. They were small, but they could come in handy.

He won't need them anymore.

She took them, buckling the sheath strips to her own calves. Each belt held three thin blades.

Machete Mama moved on, keeping just inside the tree line. She knew there would be more guards since she was so close to the lodge.

And she was correct. She found two more in the backyard, chatting about the heat and how much they hated being on lookout.

"It's not like a bitch mom is anything we should have to worry about," said the shorter of the two. "She's like five-feet-tall or some shit. I don't get why everyone's acting like Rambo is comin' after us."

"You didn't see what the whore did to Trent. Cut his fucking head off, man."

"Bullshit. Ain't no way that tiny bitch from those movies could do that. She probably had guys do it for her. Her stunt double or some shit."

"Charlie said she did all her own st—!" His words were interrupted by the machete tearing through his mouth and knocking teeth out of its way.

The shorter guy stared, mouth agape. Blood smacking his face, he fumbled for the rifle he held, but his arms seemed to have stiffened and were unable to work right.

With Ashley sticking through the back of the other guy's head, Machete Mama threw Anna. She flipped twice before punching into the shorter one's forehead. The impact threw him on his back.

There was no way of knowing for sure if that was where they were keeping her youngest daughter. But if she had to speculate, she would say it was a good chance that was where she was.

Under the breakdown process.

Machete Mama had to get out there right away. But there was a lot of ground to cross and definitely people to kill along the way.

She slipped back into the trees, sticking to the darker patches for the coverage they provided her. Every now and then, her foot came down on a brittle leaf or twig, crunching it. She'd pause, give herself time to make sure nobody was coming to investigate, then get moving again.

As she reached the edge of the woods, she saw another guard. He stood at an angle, unzipping his pants. He was young, probably in his twenties, with hair slicked back into a silky ponytail. He wore a green T-shirt and matching cargo pants.

He pulled out his penis and started to piss.

"Sweet mercy," he said through a sigh. "That's better."

The stream shooting from him was thick and yellow, spattering the ground like paint being dumped from a bucket. The loud patters covered any noise she might've made as she snuck up behind him. Raising Ashley into the air, she turned, angling herself for the swing.

"Oh. Not done," he said, chuckling to himself as another weaker stream of piss started.

Machete Mama swung down. Since she was at least a foot shorter than Mr. Ponytail, the blade *thunked* into the back of his skull, splitting it in halves that dropped down on either shoulder. His ponytail, still held together by the tie, tumbled down his back. The pee stream turned to a hissing preparing for the attack to happen at night, not the middle of the day.

She had that in her favor.

"About ready to keep moving, girls?" She looked down at the blades, saw her daughters' names scratched in the sides. Blood slipped into the scuff marks.

Looking out at the location again, she spotted another guard walking out from behind the lodge. He carried an assault rifle. Even from where she was, it looked massive. Her eyes continued to roam, moving up, scanning.

And spotted a smaller building further out from the lodge. Two guards stood by it, both armed. The building was made of logs, with a door that could have been stripped out of a dungeon attached to the front. A small, barred window was in the door, but nowhere else.

Isolation. Solitary confinement.

She thought of her movies again, exploring through the plots of each one in her head. She found the one she was looking for.

Machete Force.

The one with the human trafficking subplot. She remembered the scenes where the bad guys had taken the young girl in the film from her family and put her in a cage away from the girls they were using in the sex trade. It was their way of breaking her down, stripping out her emotions. Taking away all her hopes and her faith.

Then they got her addicted to heroin, so she wouldn't want to run away from her suppliers. Controlling her with the drug the same way a mad scientist might use a mind control device.

Anna's out there.

Raising the Anna machete, she said, "I'm coming to get you."

"No…I mean, yeah. But there are others like me. Other girls."

"Where?"

"The barn."

"The what?"

"They're in the barn, locked in stables."

Penny couldn't believe what she'd just heard. "Stables?"

"Yeah. When men show up, they go out there and choose the girl they want. Then they take them to the lodge and…you know. Charlie showed me my stable." She sniffled. "The last girl before me didn't adapt, he said. They…killed her."

Penny nodded. "When I'm through here, I'll call for help and…"

"No. We have to help them *now*."

"You can't. You need to get to Misty's. They're bound to notice their dead men soon. They'll come after me, and I don't want you to be anywhere around me when they do."

"I'll just go to the barn myself."

"You will not. You'll do what I say, Anna. I'm not losing my other daughter. For anybody. Not even those other girls."

Anna looked shocked.

Penny sighed. "I didn't mean it like that. I…" How could she remedy what she'd just said?

"Please, Mom. Please."

"Damn it." She stood up and walked back to the door. She glanced around. Things were still clear, but they wouldn't be for much longer. She slipped out and pulled off one of the dead men's T-shirts. There were a few traces of blood on it, but the other guy's shirt was doused, so it was definitely the better of the two.

She tossed the shirt to Anna. "Put that on. You've got five seconds, or we're not going to help them. I'll drag you to the woods myself."

"Mom?" Anna, confused, shoved her arms through the sleeves.

Penny had been pulled away again.

It was Machete Mama's turn.

22

The barn was in a clear patch of land settled between thick barriers of woods. A wooden fence surrounded the field behind it, attached to the back of the barn to create an area for grazing. At one point in time, this whole area had probably been used for farming. Maybe an old farmhouse had once been standing somewhere in one of the clearings. Now it was a human trafficking operation, an ugly package wrapped in pastoral beauty's wrapping paper.

Another metal door like the one on the shed had been added to the barn's front, replacing the standard swinging design all barns usually had. Four guards were there, standing around.

And Machete Mama recognized two of them.

Tommy and Eric.

They seemed to be expecting her from the way they were assembled at the front. Tommy and Eric, dressed in their deputy uniforms, were off to one side, and the two others to the other side in camouflage.

She grabbed Anna's arm and jerked her behind a tree. "Wait here." Before Anna could argue, Machete Mama put her hand to Anna's mouth, covering it with three fingers. "Do what I say."

Anna nodded. Her lips slid against her fingers.

Taking her hand away, she raised her knee. She balanced herself on one foot while she removed two of the other small blades she'd stolen from the other sheath. She put them in one hand, turning the grips so the blades faced upward behind her forearm like chopsticks. Then she stepped out onto the path and resumed walking toward the barn.

One of the unknown guards went for his gun, but Tommy stopped him. "Nah. Don't. We're supposed to take her alive. Lady Striker's orders." Stepping forward, Tommy smiled. "You look good for somebody that was killed and buried."

Machete Mama sauntered forward, bringing her hips side to side. "Death wasn't really for me, you know? Retribution is much better."

Tommy kept smiling. "You're fuckin' hot. That ass of yours..." He moaned. "I hope I get another go at it."

"You won't."

"We'll see." He looked past her, then put his eyes on her again. "We already saw your girl was with you. So, you get rid of those machetes on your sexy legs, and there won't be no trouble with her. Understand?"

"I understand. But *you* don't seem to."

"What don't I understand, beautiful?"

"You're about to die."

Tommy laughed. He elbowed Eric, who joined in, reminding her of that night at the gas station when they'd clucked with dumb encouragement for Levi.

"She sure is something," said Eric. He ran his hand through his hair, pushing it away from his eyes.

"You have no idea," said Machete Mama. She looked at the other two guards. "I'm not really into crowds, you know? Sorry, fellas. This is just between the three of us." She spun around and shot her arm out. The two blades soared, whistling as they cut through the air. The whistle ended with twin chunking sounds when they stabbed into the other guys' foreheads. One dropped right away. The other staggered a few steps, mouth hanging open and eyes crossed, before falling forward. He hit the ground with a loud thud. The hilt pounded the ground, shoving the blade even deeper into his head.

"Holy shit!" said Eric. He looked down at the dead bodies, then back up and screamed.

Smiling at him, Machete Mama had already closed the distance between them and was launching herself. Fully extended, she spiral flipped into the air. Twirling over their heads, she landed behind them and hit each guy with a punch.

Eric stumbled into Tommy, then was shoved back. "Watch it!" Tommy yelled.

"Fuck you!" Eric was about to throw a punch at Tommy.

Holding up his hands, he pointed at Machete Mama. "Not me, dumbass! Her!" He started screaming when Machete Mama grabbed his index finger and snapped it. He held up his hand and screamed louder when he saw he was now pointing at himself.

Eric surprised her with a kick to the back. She lurched forward, bashing a shoulder into the solid steel door. The look on his face showed he was just as surprised as her. He celebrated briefly before coming towards her again. This time, she wasn't distracted and evaded his kick. His foot whammed the steel, rattling the door in its frame.

Machete Mama came down with her elbow, snapping his leg at the knee with an awful crunch.

Now Eric was screaming along with Tommy while hopping on one foot.

Tommy saw this and rage washed over his face. He reached behind his back with his good hand and came back with a pair of nunchakus, chain rattling as the baton glanced off Machete Mama's shoulder. There wasn't much pain because he hadn't angled the assault correctly.

"Didn't know I could chuck, did you, bitch?"

"Don't call it that!" She jumped up, bringing her knee against his chin. He came back at her, swinging the nunchakus at her face. Ducking down, the baton hit the steel door and exploded into a ball of splinters that shot back into Tommy's face. Screaming, he flung himself away. His face looked as if he'd dunked his head in a barrel of toothpicks.

Machete Mama brandished Ashley, then swung down, slashing both of Tommy's thighs in one swing, rendering him no longer a threat. She'd severed his quads, so he wasn't getting up.

She focused on Eric again. He'd fallen onto his side and was dragging himself along the ground in a poor attempt to flee.

"Going somewhere?" she said, walking over to him.

"Look, lady! I just did what I was told!"

"You raped my daughters."

"Only one!" He winced. "I mean...no! I didn't! They told me to!"

"They told you to enjoy it?"

Eric used both arms now, digging his elbows into the ground and pulling. He didn't answer, so Machete Mama raked the Ashley blade across his back, splitting his shirt and the skin beneath it. As it stretched, she glimpsed his spine just before blood flooded the gash and hid it.

Screaming, Eric rolled onto his side and swatted at his wound. He couldn't reach it, which only seemed to make him scream more.

"Don't worry," she said. "You won't be able to feel it for much longer. I hit the main nerve, disconnecting it from the spine *almost* entirely. It's just dangling there now by the thinnest thread. It'll come loose, and then you won't be able to move at all. Quickly after that, your lungs will start to swell because you won't be able to breathe."

Eric had stopped moving. His mouth was stretched wide, his eyes bulging. She could see the panic in them, the fear of his looming death.

"Oh, looks like it's already happening. You know what *is* working, though the rest of your body isn't? Your ears. And your mind. You can't feel it happening, but you *know* it is. And isn't that just as bad? Maybe it's even worse."

The light in Eric's eyes faded.

He was dead.

Machete Mama turned around and smiled at Tommy. He hadn't moved from where he landed on his knees. His thighs had matching gashes that had spilled blood down his legs, soaking his pants.

He saw her looking at him. "You're a fucked up bitch!"

"You fucked me up," she said, ambling toward him, holding out Ashley so the blood could run off the tip. "You and Charlie and the rest just fucked me up even more than I already was."

"Lady Striker's gonna kill your ass. You're gonna pay…"

"I've already paid way more than I owed, Tommy. I've come to take some of it back." She stepped around to the side of him, raised her foot, and placed the boot against the back of his head. "What was that you said back in the bedroom?"

"Huh? What?"

"Didn't you ask to roll me over?" She shoved the back of his head with her foot. He dropped forward, catching himself on his hands.

Head whipping, his breathing went fast and squeaky. "What are you doing?"

"I want to fuck you in the ass, Tommy."

Tommy started to scream even before she rammed the blade between his buttocks. But when the machete plunged, his screams hit a frequency she'd never heard come from a person before. She twisted the blade back, angling it so it would travel upward and not go out the front. She figured it was in his stomach now, jabbing his insides. She wrenched the blade out, grimacing at the chunky blood falling off, then slammed it back in three quick times. She tugged down, ripping him open between his legs and removing the machete.

Tommy collapsed. He was no longer screaming. The sounds coming from him were not unlike the puling a dying cow might make. She wiped Ashley clean on his back, then put her away.

Leaving him there, she walked over to the steel door and tugged. It was locked. She found the keys on Eric and unlocked it, then threw the door aside. It rumbled on its rollers, allowing light to enter. Unlike the shed, there was meager illumination from lamps attached to the walls.

Every stable door was open.

"Hello?" she called.

Nobody responded. That wasn't surprising. These poor girls had been programmed not to speak to anyone, to not run away.

"I'm here to help you," she said, going inside. It was hot and stuffy, with the odor of a petting zoo hanging in the air.

As she approached the first stable, she looked this way and that. There weren't many spots somebody could hide in. So, she doubted anybody was about to jump out at her. Which was also a little odd. Whether the girls would risk fleeing or not, there should've been at least one guard inside making sure they didn't try anything while she was outside fighting the others.

She reached the first stable and looked inside. "Shit."

The girl had been pretty, that much she could tell. The bullet hole in her head hadn't taken that from her. Machete Mama moved down to the next stable and found another dead girl. Though she figured she would find dead girls in every stall, she checked anyway and wasn't surprised. The one that hurt her the most was the girl who couldn't have been any older than twelve. Not only had she been put through whatever despicable nightmare that being a captive had presented, she'd been coldly executed.

That's what they'd been doing out here.

Probably had just finished when Machete Mama showed up.

If I hadn't argued with Anna. If I'd just come out here soon as she'd said it...

Penny started to filter through Machete Mama's mechanical conscience. The heartache was profound as it seemed to take over everything. She saw all these dead girls and knew there were mothers who'd never get their daughters returned to them.

Just like Ashley.

Just like me.

Tears spilled down her cheeks.

Stop crying!

She couldn't. Standing there in the barn of the dead, Machete Mama sobbed. Her shoulders jerked and twitched as she wept harder than she probably ever had in all her life. She felt Alex's death all over again, but without the border she'd built around herself to shield her from grief. She felt Ashley's death again, felt the brutal emptiness and loss that had weakened her and made her lose her fight against Lady Striker.

And now, all these poor girls. She felt the death of each one, though she hadn't personally known any of them. She felt the misery of several mothers all at once, ripping her heart into pieces.

Soon, the pain began to fade. It didn't go away completely, but seemed to attach somewhere deep inside her, becoming part of her inner structure. It found a home alongside the rage, the anger, the hate, and yet, it was somehow neighbors with her compassion, her empathy, and her love.

All of it was now what made her. She'd been shattered, broken, and had been rebuilt into a new Machete Mama. One that somehow coexisted with Penny Chambers.

They were one.

"Anna."

She couldn't let her daughter see this. The shock would be too much.

Runing out of the barn, she squinted against the harsh sunlight. She ran over to the trees and found the one she told Anna to wait behind.

But she was gone.

23

"Anna!" She spun circles, eyes combing the woods. She didn't see her daughter anywhere. "*Anna!*"

"*Mom—ow!*"

Her voice had come from further away. Penny bolted, making her way back up the dirt path they'd taken on their way to the barn. She hadn't gone far when she found her daughter again. And she wasn't alone.

"Look familiar?" asked Charlie.

He stood behind her, wearing his uniform, and pressed against Anna's backside. His face was nestled in her tangled hair as his nose moved up and down, sniffing her. Just like he had been at the cabin when he brought Anna into the bedroom.

His hand reached up, squeezing her breast through the green T-shirt. It stretched taught over the mound. "Even after being locked in a shed and having to shit in a bucket, she still smells like damn fruit. And I want to eat from the forbidden tree."

Anna began to cry.

"Let her go, Charlie."

"Let her go? You think I could even if I wanted to? She's supposed to be dead now. Lady Striker gave me the order to kill 'em all, even little cutie here."

"That's why the other girls are dead?"

Anna whimpered hearing that.

Charlie nodded. "The boss ain't been right since we found Trent. Between you and me, she's gettin' a little paranoid."

"Covering her tracks."

"Shuttin' down. For now. So, the girls have to go."

"You hurt Anna anymore, I'll kill you."

"Didn't you come here to kill me, anyway? Are any of the boys left? Did you get them all?"

"I'm pretty sure you're all that's left."

"Until the night crew comes in. Which they should be starting to file in within the hour to start their shifts. You're good, but I doubt you can take on twenty at once."

"I just want to take on you, Charlie. Show me you got a pair of your own. Let her go and face me."

Charlie laughed. "You know I got a pair. I fucked you hard with what I got."

"Now it's time for you to see what I got. Let her go. Let's do this." She rolled her hands, performing her kata, and took her stance."

"I can't kill you. Lady Striker forbids it. But I guess I can fuck you up some." He put his mouth against Anna's ear. "Want to watch me beat the shit out of your mother?"

Anna, wincing, tried to pull her face away.

He shoved her aside. She fell to the ground and moaned. Though seeing her daughter get roughly manhandled like that made her boil inside, she didn't allow it to influence her actions. She stood there, keeping her stance, and did not move.

But her eyes glanced down and saw the small chainsaws dangling from each of his hips, attached to hoops on his belt.

"Ah," he said. "I see you looking." He put a hand on each one as if he were a lumberjack gunslinger, then ripped them from their hoops. "I thought long and hard about this because I knew one day you and I would face each other. I mean, it was inevitable. Soon as Lady Striker told me the plan to get you to come back to town, I knew our confrontation was coming. But I wanted a hook, you know. My own cool name, too. You remember how my dad used to do landscaping? Well, I got pretty good with a chainsaw, working with him on the weekends and summer breaks. They even had a nickname for me on the crew.

"They called me Chainsaw Charlie."

He put the tops of the chainsaws together, hooked the grips of the pully cords together, and yanked his arms down in opposite directions. The pully cords extended. Each motor brattled to life, chains spinning.

"Oh, fuck me," said Machete Mama, drawing her machetes.

Charlie let out a growl and charged at her, swinging the saws. Machete Mama did a back flip, avoiding the first swing, then cartwheeled sideways to avoid another attack. He came back with a kick that caught her in the breasts and knocked her breath out. Her vision began to dip.

"Mom!" Anna yelled, pulling Machete Mama out of her foggy mind in time to see the chainsaw coming for her chest. She brought up the Anna blade, blocking it. Metal screeched with a spray of sparks.

Charlie howled, then swung the other saw at her. She bent backwards, watching the spinning blade slide past her face. Strands of her hair were sliced off and fluttered away.

Machete Mama turned and kicked out behind her, bending her leg so her foot landed between his shoulder blades. He let out a grunt and staggered, swinging back with his right hand, the throttle wide open on the chainsaw.

She felt the wind in her face before twirling away. She started to raise her machetes, but pain in her right arm caught her attention. She was shocked to find a serrated split on her shoulder that was caused by a chainsaw blade. Blood was oozing out in lines on her skin.

"Gotcha!" Charlie yelled. He ran at her, bringing up both saws.

Machete Mama stepped into his momentum, surprising him. She brought her leg up, giving three quick kicks against the side of his head. Then she pulled her foot back and planted another one on his nose. Even over the brattling motors, she heard the crunch of bone and felt his nose cave under her boot.

Still, he didn't go down.

Nose flat on his face and gushing blood from his mashed nostrils, he ran at her, growling. His eyes were big and white inside the crimson mask.

She swung the machetes up, hitting the chains and crying out as hot sparks sprinkled across her face. Charlie slammed into her, lifted her off her feet, and bucked with his shoulders. She tumbled over him, dropping behind his back. She managed to get her feet under her before she landed. If she hadn't, she would have wound up on her back, and Charlie could've finished her off. But she was able to leap backwards, performing a flip low to the ground. She landed in a split and swung in with both machetes. Her plan had been to chop off each leg.

But Charlie blocked them with the chainsaws. More sparks rained down while she whipped her legs back together and springboarded back to her feet.

Charlie was grinning through the blood now. He was feeling more confident, and Machete Mama couldn't blame him for it. She was on the verge of losing. But his vanity was going to do him in.

"I've got a rock-hard boner right now," he said. "I'm gonna use blood for lube and fuck that ass again."

"Come get it," she said, holding the machetes up and forming an X in front of her.

Laughing, Charlie ran at her. If she didn't time this just right, he would plow through her. She needed to make sure that—

Charlie kicked dirt into her face, blinding her.

Each time she blinked, she felt the hard grit under her lids. His laughter rose above the revving motors, and that told her where he was. She managed to pull her head back, heard the chains grind together when they connected. Hot, oil-tinged air buffeted her face.

She kept blinking, letting the tears cleanse her eyes. She was able to catch a blurry shape moving toward her. It shook like a reflection in a puddle. The roaring chainsaws filled her ears. She blinked again and could see Charlie even better.

He was bringing a saw down to her arm.

In a panic, Machete Mama swung up with the other arm, putting Ashley between the chainsaw and the arm gripping the Anna machete. This time, there was a big burst of sparks that flecked her skin with hot spots.

Charlie stumbled back, which allotted Machete Mama the chance to dig her knee into the dirt. She spun on it, swinging out with Anna and slashed his stomach, carving a grin in his abdomen. Charlie cried out, then thrust the chainsaws, hitting the machetes, and knocking them from her hands.

She held up her empty hands and gasped at the trembling pain she felt in both. Standing over her, Charlie laughed. "You got me good, but I just got you better."

"I meant to drop them, Charlie. And you fell for it." She grinned. "Idiot."

Charlie frowned.

She punched the slit in his stomach. Her fist vanished inside him, sinking halfway up her forearm, past the bandage on her older wound. Screaming, Charlie tried to raise the chainsaws, but the strength was leaving his arms. He dropped one. It shut off when it hit the ground.

She dug around his insides, gripped a greasy tube of intestine, and yanked it through the flaps of his flesh. Holding onto it, she sprinted up his torso and jumped over his head, tugging out a length of his guts with her. Landing behind him, she wrapped the rope around his neck a few times and pulled.

Charlie's head wrenched back. She kicked him behind the knees, bringing him down. As he started to fall forward, she planted her boot in the small of his back and heaved, torquing his body backward over her extended leg while she strangled him with his own intestines.

Dropping the other chainsaw, he reached out with both arms, swatting the air as if trying to hit her. He didn't come close. With both chainsaws shut off, she was able to hear his terror through his quacking grunts. It was a wonderful opus of music that filled her with satisfaction. He clawed at the lumpy innards squeezing his throat. Slapped them. Tried to stick his fingers behind them.

He could do nothing.

She coiled the intestines around her hand and forearm for a tighter grip and jerked as hard as she could. Charlie's head shot back. There was a snap, then his head was able to touch his back. Upside down, his face was slack as his dead eyes gazed back at her. She puckered her lips at him, untangled her hand from his guts, and let him drop onto his stomach.

Machete Mama leaned back and let out a drawn-out battle cry, releasing the fury she'd been holding onto. It faded from her lungs, as did the reverberating retort in the air. Lowering her head, she took deep breaths, steeling herself.

After a few moments, she looked at Anna. Her youngest daughter had pulled her bare legs to her chest and was hugging them. Trembling, her dirty hair hung over her face as she stared out through the messy curtain of curls.

There was pure fear in her eyes.

Machete Mama melted inside. "Anna?"

Anna flinched. She took a quivery breath. "You-you-you…ripped…you…choked him…"

She's going into shock.

"Anna." She snapped her fingers once. It worked. "Listen to me." She stepped over to Charlie. She was about to reach for him, then saw the glove of Charlie's blood coating hand. Using the other cleaner hand, she unhooked the keys from his belt and tossed them. They landed at Anna's feet. "Go down the hill. Charlie's cruiser is down there in the clearing. I'm sure it has a GPS. Put this in it and go there." She told her the address. "Can you remember that?"

Anna stared at the keys as if she'd never seen such things before. She raised her shivering head. "Huh?"

"Did you hear any of what I said?"

"Um…" Her eyes moved down.

"Don't look at him, Anna. Look at me." Anna lifted her gaze back to Machete Mama. "Did you hear what I said?"

Anna nodded. "Yuh-yeah."

"Repeat the address to me." Anna did. "That's my girl. That's my friend's house. Misty. Remember, I told you about her earlier? She knows what's going on. Drive there in Charlie's cruiser. Okay? Misty will help you. She'll protect you until I get back."

"You're not coming with me?"

Shaking her head, she turned and looked up. The mountain peak towered over them as the sun was starting to slip behind it. "I have to go somewhere else. Get going."

"Will you walk me down? Make sure I…?"

Machete Mama shook her head again. "No. But take your sister with you. Just in case." She held out the Ashley machete to Anna.

"My sister?" Her eyes locked on the engraved name. "Jesus…"

"Get going. Now."

She helped Anna stand up. "What are you gonna do, Mom?"

"I'm going to leave a message for Lady Striker. Go. I love you." She hugged Anna, then gave her a gentle push to get her moving. "Be careful. I love you."

Looking over her shoulder, Anna said, "I love you, too. Tears had washed lines through the dirt on her face. "Please…come back to me…"

"I promise I will."

She waited until Anna was out of sight, then she shoved her hand inside Charlie's stomach again. When it was immersed in his blood, she pulled it back out and used her bloody fingers to draw the image of two crossing machetes on Charlie's torso. She'd painted a similar image on the wall of a drug dealer's house in *Machete Law* with corn syrup blood. The fake stuff could look close to the real thing, but genuine blood felt completely different.

When her bloody artwork was complete, she grabbed one of his chainsaws and stabbed the blade into the ground. Then she took Charlie's arm, extended his finger, and placed his hand on top of the chainsaw's bulky body jutting from the dirt. Leaning down, she closed one eye and checked where his finger was pointing.

She smiled.

The extended digit lined up perfectly with the top of the mountain.

24

The moon looked close enough to jump onto from the top of the mountain. Penny stared out at the rocky orb, tracing the outlines of battle scars from constant poundings of asteroids and meteors. Much like Machete Mama, its wounds were a grim manifestation of its past.

Sitting cross-legged near the ledge, she let her mind drift into the sky and mend with the stars. She could see each one up close, in full detail as if they were projected inside her.

Alex's face was among them, connected by the twinkling dots. He was watching her.

"Alex?" she said.

His face faded as he began to smile. She loved it when he appeared like that, but hated to see him go. It hurt her every time, as it had the first time he left her.

The hike up the mountain took almost three hours. It would have been a shorter expedition, but she'd come across a stream and soaked in it. Then she drank. The cold water had cleaned her and refreshed her.

By the time she reached the top, her shoulder had bled down her arm again, creating a crimson sleeve. At times, the pain was able to get through the hedge of protection she'd built around herself. But each time, she was able to push it away and keep it from affecting her.

The horrified expression on Anna's face kept showing itself. She'd seen fear in her own daughter's eyes. Fear that was directed at Penny, that had been caused by her.

Her own daughter was afraid of her.

No. Machete Mama.

"We're the same," she said in a quiet voice.

Anna had been through so much, had seen so much. Would she ever be able to look at her own mother the way she used to? Would their relationship ever be able to recover?

When would Anna start to blame her for Ashley's death?

God. It is my fault.

She hadn't made sure Lady Striker was dead. And she'd come back. Ashley was dead because Penny had been sloppy, had taken pity on the defeated woman.

When Anna realizes that, she'll hate me forever.

Maybe she should be hated. There was no way Anna would ever be able to view Penny as the same woman who'd raised her. She would always have that fear somewhere inside of her, expecting any moment for the same woman who'd ripped out a man's guts to show herself again.

Penny gritted her teeth. She couldn't let such thoughts distract her. Not right now. These were issues that she could worry about later. In fact, it was time for Machete Mama to take the driver's seat again. Penny would slide over to the passenger seat, a part of the journey but not the captain.

A twig snapped in the woods. All sounds halted as mother nature held her breath.

"There you are," she said.

"So much for the element of surprise," said Lady Striker.

Machete Mama rose to her feet, her back arched. She turned around.

Lady Striker stood at the launch of the clearing. All her weight was on one foot, jutting a hip. A sai was in each hand, their blades pointing out. Her long hair fluttered in the howling wind. Being up so high and without anything to shield the strong gusts, it felt as if it could carry them away.

Machete Mama slid Anna out of her sheath.

"You only have one now?" asked Lady Striker.

"It's all I need." Lady Striker's smirk was easy to see in the washed-out moonlight on her face. "I see you got my message."

"Was hard to miss. You killed them all—Charlie, Trent, Tommy, Eric, and Levi. Got all the bad boys that hurt you and your girls. Making them wrongs right. Retribution. Justice served."

"Not completely. There's still you."

"Me." She nodded. "Me. It's always been me. I've always been the demon in the shadows of your life. I'm your ghost."

Machete Mama nodded. "You haunt me."

"And you haunt me. You're *my* ghost. I should've known I didn't kill you back at the cabin because you were still in my nightmares. Still waving your machetes in my face. I can't truly live again until you die, truly live. I'm a zombie under your fucking voodoo curse. You control everything in here." She tapped the side of her head with a sai. "I want to be free of you, Machete Mama. I want to break the chains that bind us together."

"So do I."

"But I'm scared."

"Scared?"

"What will I do when I no longer have you to hate? When the fantasy of your death becomes a reality, what will drive me? What will my focus be? All these years, everything I've done has been leading me here. When I've killed you, what do I do next?"

"Only one way to find out." Machete Mama stretched out her leg, digging her heel into the dirt. She brought Anna up, ignoring the throbbing in her shoulder.

"Only one way," said Lady Striker.

She broke into a sprint, raising both sais in her fists. The blade and sai guards stuck out like claws. Machete Mama launched herself using her planted foot. She ran a few feet and leaped just as Lady Striker leaped. Bodies rising, the full moon shone behind them like the eye of a god watching their ultimate battle.

They collided in the air with a clang. Machete Mama felt a hot blast of pain in her chest. She soared past, landing on her feet on the opposite side of the ground. Looking down, she saw a long slice on the bare skin of her chest between the tank top straps.

Shit...she got me.

There was blood on Anna also, a pale streak sliding down the blade. She turned around. Lady Striker was coming for another attack. Her side was bloody, the leather corset ripped.

Got you, too!

Machete Mama jumped back, dodging the sais, and threw a forearm uppercut. She caught Lady Striker's chin, clacking her teeth together. Then she cried out as the sai raked her stomach, tearing the tank top open and slicing across the stitches underneath, ripping away the bandages.

"So much for letting that heal," said Lady Striker, laughing. She spit out a tooth, then pounded the sai's head into Machete Mama's stomach.

Machete Mama was already in a bad spot. If she didn't stop this assault, all her wounds would be reopened, and she'd quickly bleed out.

She blocked the next sai hit and brought the machete up. Her plan had been to block the other hit, but Lady Striker was already rushing closer. She was being sloppy, but Machete Mama was grateful for it because Anna slashed the exposed armpit. Lady Striker squealed, pulling her arm back down. Machete Mama chopped her neck with her free hand, then shoved her back.

An arm to her throat, Lady Striker lurched. A sai blade shot at Machete Mama's face. She turned her head, just missing the jab. She sank her teeth into the skin of Lady Striker's forearm and tore out a chunk. She spit it out, then kicked Lady Striker in the chest as her adversary screamed in pain.

Lady Striker held up her arm. A ragged hole was in the meat, spurting blood. She'd lost the sai she'd been holding in that hand. "You bit my arm?"

Machete Mama backhanded the blood from her mouth. "I was going for your neck."

"Bitch." She jumped, flipping over, her legs fully extended as she made a circle through the air. The sai shot out.

Machete Mama hacked it away, jumping in the other direction. Both women landed at the same time and went straight back to offensive maneuvers. Their blades clanged. The machete had slipped between the sai's blade and guard. Lady Striker flicked her wrist, locking it in place.

She's trying to break Anna!

Machete Mama twisted her hand the other way, but the blade wouldn't dislodge. She kicked at Lady Striker's face. Missed. As she brought her leg down, Lady Striker stepped forward and brought her fist up in a hard strike on Machete Mama's elbow.

Pain blasted through her arm, then a tingling numbness took hold. Machete Mama couldn't hold on to Anna anymore. Releasing the machete, she staggered back, unarmed.

"Now what're you gonna do?" said Lady Striker. She flung her arm. The machete flew from the sai, stabbing into the ground a few away. It might as well have been tossed off the mountain because Machete Mama couldn't go for it with Lady Striker blocking her way.

Her opponent lunged, jabbing with the sai. Machete Mama pulled back, ducked, turned, and ducked again to avoid being stabbed. When Lady Striker came close for another series of attacks, Machete Mama caught her arm with both hands, twirled around, and yanked down.

Lady Striker's arm snapped over Machete Mama's shoulder.

Shrieking, Lady Striker dropped the sai. Machete Mama caught it, spun around, and thrust her arm toward the other woman's chest. Lady Striker bent at the hip sideways, going under the blade, then planted a fist in Machete Mama's bleeding stomach.

As Machete Mama tottered back, Lady Striker backtracked, snatched Anna from the ground, and turned back around. Her right arm dangled at an odd angle. "This works…killing you with your own machete. Artsy way to go out. Poetic."

Machete Mama saw the other sai, bent over to pick it up, and held them both up. "You only have one," she said, throwing Lady Striker's words back at her.

Lady Striker's smile sank. "I only need one."

Machete Mama didn't like hearing her own words in retort.

They ran at each other again, yelling. Steel clamored as weapons collided and attacks were thwarted. The women grunted and screamed in each other's faces, caught each other with elbows, kicks, and even a headbutt or two.

Lady Striker spun her broken arm like a club and nailed Machete Mama's aching stomach. The blow folded her over with an exhale of air. She brought her long leg up, extended it, and swung it down in a scissor kick across the back of Machete Mama's neck.

Machete Mama was on the ground with no memory of getting there. She could hear Lady Striker's movements, coming closer with a cry. She rolled out of the way as a boot stomped the ground where her head had been. Getting on her back, she saw the boot was already coming back down again. She rolled again and again as the stomps kept coming, avoiding each one. After the fourth miss, Lady Striker screamed, then swung down with the machete.

She crossed the sais, blocking the blade. Her eyes homed in on the name scratched into the side.

Anna.

With another burst of energy, Machete Mama jumped to her feet. It was time to end this. Time for this fight to be finished, this hatred and feud to be over.

Machete Mama spun on her heel, stretching out her arms. She held a sai in each hand, angled inward. The tips of both blades were pointing out.

Lady Striker stabbed Anna into Machete Mama's stomach.

Everything went quiet except for a faint ringing in Machete Mama's ears. The world seemed to slow down, as if time had gone off track, slowing down each second to match the rapidly decreasing speed of Machete Mama's heartbeat.

Somehow, Machete Mama could see from the outside of her body, as if watching the battle through the glass of an aquarium. Eyes wide, she took a couple steps back. Anna protruded from the center of her stomach, halfway deep. Though she knew Anna hadn't done it on purpose, the hurt she felt that her daughter was causing this pain made it so much worse.

Lady Striker laughed. "Got you..." She was winded. Each time she panted, she winced, as if it hurt to breathe. "Fucking got you..."

Machete Mama could hardly stand up. Knees bobbling, her legs felt like they'd been filled with dough. She still held the sais in each hand, but Lady Striker stepped forward and took them from her without any trouble. Now, her hands were empty, and she stared at them, confused that everything had changed so quickly.

She's got me...

It was over.

It's not over. Alex's voice. *It's not over. You are not defeated. You are hurt. She has not won. Remember the scenes. Remember* Machete Fury.

"Machete...Fury...?"

Lady Striker frowned. Tilting her head, she studied Machete Mama. "What the hell are you talking about?"

The scene transitioned into her mind. She saw it as vividly as if she were in front of the cameras filming it. The crucial difference being that the sword sticking out of her then was an FX prop applied by talented artists. A rig that was fully operational for an impressive effect. One that she would have to do for real if she got the chance.

Lady Striker twirled her sais, then put them in the loops on her belt. "Don't think I didn't notice your kid's name carved in the blade. I guess the other machete had the other girl's name on it. The dead one? Ashley?"

Machete Mama's focus began to come back from the mention of her oldest daughter's name.

"That's pretty iconic," said Lady Striker. "Would've been a nice touch in the movies." She stepped closer. "I get the meaning behind it. It's noble, really. I'd feel something if I was able to feel anything at all anymore. Maybe once you're gone, I can absorb what you had. That heart. The soul inside. So bright that even now, moments before your death, it shines. Almost blindingly so. *Stubbornly* so. Why won't you die?"

Machete Mama coughed up blood. "Machete…Fury…"

"What the hell are you talking about, bitch?" Lady Striker was even closer now. "Who cares? I can't believe I get to kill you with your own weapon. It was meant to be. And that you'll die by a blade with your own daughter's name on it? Amazing." Lady Striker stood before her. She shook her head. "Feels like I've waited an eternity for this."

"Me…too…"

The scene in *Machete Fury* flashed through her mind in a flicker of images as if burnt onto bad film. She saw the villain, The Swordsman, stepping up to her just as Lady Striker had now. His sword was in the same place as Anna was. Under her shirt, the FX artist had built a rig that had a fake blade attached to her back. It was folded down, mounted to a spring that, when triggered, would cause it to pop out.

Penny Chambers had been instructed by Earl Karlson, the FX artist, to spin around and step up to The Swordsman.

Machete Mama, on the mountaintop, followed the same orders. Her sudden movement caught Lady Striker by surprise, just as it was scripted to do to The Swordsman.

"Now, grip the handle with both hands," he'd told Penny Chambers. His long hair was pulled back in a messy ponytail that was streaked with gray. "You have to push down on it hard enough to trigger the release." His midwestern accent was strong and always amused her.

Machete Mama gripped Anna's hilt with both hands and leaned over as she pushed.

In the scene, the spring clapped, and the fake blade burst from her back, retracting when it pushed against The Swordsman's stomach.

But the blade that ripped through Machete Mama's back was real and slicked in her *real* blood. It punched into Lady Striker's stomach, sinking all the way in and pinning them together.

Lady Striker choked out a groan in Machete Mama's ear.

Pain pulsed through Machete Mama, causing her vision to darken. Gripping the machete, she pulled, wrenching Anna from their stomachs. Blood shot from Lady Striker's mouth and rained onto Machete Mama's shoulder, thick and warm.

She shuffled forward, moving like a zombie, and turned around as Lady Striker dropped to her knees in front of her. Hugging herself, she looked up at Machete Mama. Blood trailed from both corners of her mouth, coating her chin.

"How…?" she coughed, spitting up thick clumps of blood. "How…are you so…strong?"

Machete Mama took a deep breath. She held Anna in one hand, pushing her other hand against the gushing stab wound in her stomach. "The Ancient Ones…"

Lady Striker nodded. "They abandoned me."

"You abandoned them first."

Lady Striker moved her arms, looking down at her bleeding stomach. Her leather shorts were shiny with blood, her thighs streaked in red. "Fuck. You won."

"Not…yet." Machete Mama stepped forward. "Remember what you said?"

Lady Striker's eyes narrowed as she thought about it. Then her face relaxed. "I remember."

"I should've cut off your head."

Machete Mama swung the machete with the last of her strength, lopping off Lady Striker's head. It twirled away in the darkness, leaving the body on its knees, spurting thick ropy lines of blood from the neck stump. As the pressure of the squirts began to abate, the body pitched forward onto the dirt.

She stared down at Lady Striker's dead body. "Now…I've won."

It was hard, but she stayed on her feet while she wiped the blood off Anna on Lady Striker's bare leg. Then she slid her into the sheath and walked away.

She hadn't gone very far before she collapsed.

25

"Am I under arrest or not?" Penny finished buttoning the flannel shirt Misty had brought her to wear for her release from the hospital. She'd been cooped up in this room for most of the summer after being in a coma for two weeks, finally awakening in a room with Anna sleeping in an added bed beside her, Misty in the reclining chair, and an older man in the uncomfortable extra chair in the corner. He'd reminded her of her grandfather with his white hair and matching mustache, dressed in a suit that didn't really seem to fit into any style. Right away, she pegged him for a cop, and she'd been right.

He'd been there to ask questions, and he'd asked a lot of them over the weeks since she came to. Mostly about how she'd managed to survive such unbearable wounds. Not just the ones from her final battle, but also those she'd received when Lady Striker and her boys first attacked.

"Ancient magic," she'd told him, and meant it.

And he'd believed her. He had to. After all, they found her in the woods high up in the mountains, stabbed multiple times and bleeding all over the place. She'd been unconscious and had probably been lying there on the path for three days.

Another body had been found, beheaded. That was easy to interpret because it was missing the head, though nobody had been able to recover it, which hadn't stopped bothering Penny. Where the hell had Lady Striker's head disappeared to?

"A coyote or bear probably ran off with," Lt. Stiltson had said.

Penny told him he was probably right, but she hadn't really believed that. Nor did she have any idea why she didn't. There was no way it had sprouted legs and walked off on its own. Somebody must have taken it. Who could've done such a thing? Penny had no idea. Nor could she speculate why somebody would.

But the rest of the evidence was there on the mountain. A brutal fight had taken place, but nobody had any idea why.

Not until Penny woke up. And that was why Detective Lieutenant John Stiltson had been camping out in the room with Anna and Misty off and on through the weeks. He'd wanted to be there when Penny came out of the coma.

Yes, the detective had lots of questions. And Penny had lots of answers.

Now Stiltson stood with his back to her. "Are you decent yet?"

Penny buttoned the final button, leaving a few undone around her neck. The stitches from the sai slash had dissolved, leaving a pale line that looked like a snake stretched under her collarbone. Another scar that would be there forever. "Yes."

He turned around, smiled. "You look so much better. Feel better?"

"Like a million bucks," she said in a sarcastic voice. She dropped the S.A. Cosby book she'd been reading in her bag, then added the puzzle magazines Anna had given her to help keep her busy. "Anna will be here in a minute to walk with me down to the car."

"You have to be wheeled out. Policy. And the law."

"Whatever. Am I being *wheeled* out to Misty's car or a police car?"

"*Should* I arrest you?"

Penny zipped the bag. "You want me to tell you how to do your job now? Haven't I talked enough over the last few weeks?"

"You're being released from the hospital after being here for over two months. You'd think you'd be somewhat more chipper."

"A chipper mood? I have to bury my other daughter. Haven't been able to give her a proper funeral because I've been in this…place." She waved her hand around. There were still faint bruises peppered along her skin. "She's been sitting at the funeral home in Georgia, waiting for me. I…" She didn't know what point she was trying to make. The old detective's pleasant face made it hard to stay mad.

"You're alive. Anna is alive. And you two can start a new life. You can heal and deal with the loss of Ashley together."

"So, I'm *not* being arrested?"

"You single-handedly eradicated the crime syndicate that had been holding your cute small town hostage for years. Why would I arrest you for that?"

"Isn't it illegal? I killed a shitload of people."

"If word got out that it was you that did it all, that you enacted a type of private, vigilante justice with your own hands, then yes, it would be illegal. But nobody needs to know that. It's better for you, better for us, and better for the feds that the town thinks you were a victim, along with your daughters." He ran his hand through his feathered hair. "And since the local authorities and feds are going to take the credit for what you did, then I don't see why *you* should be punished for it."

"I don't want the credit. Never did. I just wanted them dead."

"And you got that. Oh, did you ever. Took a long time to gather up all the body parts."

Penny sat on the edge of the bed she'd been stuck in for several weeks. "It's really over."

"I'm glad to hear you say that. So, that means you'll be leaving town?"

She nodded. "Right away. Going to sell my aunt's cabin through a lawyer. I'm not coming back here."

"That's probably for the best. You did a great service, but I think it's probably best you stay away. Forever."

"Agreed."

"For what it's worth, I hate what happened to you. All of it. Nobody should have to endure what all you've been through."

Penny nodded again. She didn't trust herself to speak.

There was a light knock at the door. Anna peeked her head in. "Safe to come in?"

Stiltson smiled. He always seemed to blush a little whenever Anna came around. It wasn't a weird kind of blush, but more like the kind Penny's own grandfather would do when she was small. He was genuinely glad to see her. "Perfectly safe. I was just leaving."

He walked past Anna, gave her another smile, and headed to the door. He paused. "Take care of yourself, Mrs. Chambers."

"I will."

He left them alone.

Anna looked at her, her smile weakening. "Are you okay?" Her face had healed nicely. Misty had taken her to get her hair done a couple weeks ago, getting it trimmed and styled in a different way with layers. It looked good on her, making her look older and youthful all at the same time.

"She looks like a younger you," Misty had said.

Penny had to agree because it felt like she was looking at herself at seventeen.

"I *will* be okay as soon as I'm out of here," Penny said.

"The nurse is outside with your chariot."

"My wheelchair."

"Well, that doesn't sound as fancy as a chariot. Just pretend it's one without the horses."

Penny waited for the nurse to roll the chair over to the bed. She stood up, handed her bag to Anna, and sat down. The nurse leaned over and folded down the footrests. She put her feet in them and smiled again at the new shoes Anna had picked out for her. They looked like something a teenager would wear.

Outside, the sun was hot and bright. Summer was in its last humid sprint as it neared the end of August. Fall would be here soon, which would make the mountain areas look gorgeous with the foliage turning an array of bright colors. But Penny wouldn't be here to see it, and she was just fine with that.

Misty stood at the back of her SUV parked by the curb, wearing sunglasses and smiling. Penny was glad her old friend had started smiling at her again. It had taken a while for her to forgive Penny for forcing her to pass out and leaving her behind. She understood why she'd done such a cruel trick, but as Misty had said in the hospital room one night, she didn't like that Penny had been out there fighting an army by herself.

"There's the sunshine," said Misty.

Penny smirked. "Right."

"Can you go from here?" the nurse asked.

"I could've gone the whole way," she said, standing.

The nurse took the wheelchair back inside.

Penny walked over to the SUV just as Anna put her bag in the back. A case was also back there, black vinyl and shiny, like something a gangster might use to carry money in. "What's that?"

"Aww, you saw your gift already."

"My gift?"

"Yeah." Misty stepped over to the case, looked around, and unlocked the clasps. Raising the lid, she said, "Got them cleaned up and sharpened. Got you this new case to keep them in."

Ashley was tucked into the foam padding of the lid Misty held. Anna was in the lower section, cradled in matching foam. Both blades looked brand new and gleaming. The names were easier to read.

The case clicked shut.

"Like it?" asked Misty.

Penny smiled. "Love it. Thank you."

"Didn't want them to wind up buried somewhere again. Now you'll have them if you ever…well…" Misty shrugged.

Inside, the SUV felt wonderful from the air conditioning. Penny, in the passenger seat, angled the vent at her face. Cool air blew against her cheeks, drying the sweat that had already popped up from the muggy heat outside.

Anna, in the back seat, buckled her seatbelt.

"Who's ready for the road trip?" asked Misty, pulling away from the curb. "I've never been to Georgia."

"Thank you for driving us. And thank you for staying to help out with Ashley and her…" She didn't want to say it again. Saying it to Stiltson had been hard enough.

"What are friends for?"

Penny smiled. "Yeah."

"You guys are weird," said Anna from the back.

"Put in your earbuds."

"AirPods."

"Whatever."

Misty laughed. "I'm looking forward to spending time with you guys *outside* the hospital."

"How long are you going to stay with us?"

"A couple days."

"That's not long at all. You should stay longer after we handle everything."

"Yeah," said Anna. "There's plenty of room."

"I probably can stay a little longer after what needs to be done. But not much."

"Bruh," said Anna. "That's lame."

Penny rolled her eyes. "Mind my daughter's dialect."

"I'm used to it by now," said Misty. "We spent a lot of time together while you were in dreamland."

"I bet so."

Misty waited for Anna to lose herself in whatever she was listening to with her AirPods. "I have places to go. My case was back there, too, with yours. I got a matching one for myself."

Penny stared at Misty, confused at first. Then she remembered the story she'd told her that one night.

She was attacked, assaulted.

Her sledgehammer must have been back there in a case that Penny hadn't seen.

"They hauled ass out of Briarwood when the feds raided town," said Misty. "I know where to find them. It's time I do it."

Penny thought about trying to talk her out of it, but she knew nothing she said would do any good. Misty needed her own closure, needed to free herself from the prison her memories held her in. Killing the bastards who'd caused it all would take care of everything.

Penny looked over at her friend.

"Do you need my help?"

MORE TITLES FROM KRISTOPHER RUFTY!

Lurkers Go to College
Stump Juice
Lipstick Wings
Victims
Lucy
Old Scratch
Pillowface Rules
All Will Die
The Devoured and the Dead
Hell Departed: Pillowface Vs. The Lurkers
Anathema
Master of Pain
(Written with Wrath James White)
Something Violent
Seven Buried Hill
The Vampire of Plainfield
The Lurking Season
Bigfoot Beach
Desolation
Jagger
Prank Night
The Skin Show
Proud Parents
Oak Hollow
Pillowface
The Lurkers
Angel Board
Jackpot
(Written with Shane McKenzie, Adam Cesare, & David Bernstein)
Last One Alive
A Dark Autumn
Bone Chimes
Bone Chimes 2
Bone Chimes 3
Escapement

ABOUT THE AUTHOR

Kristopher Rufty lives in North Carolina with his three children and pets. He's written over twenty novels, including *Old Scratch, Pillowface Rules, All Will Die, The Devoured and the Dead, Desolation, The Vampire of Plainfield, The Lurkers,* and more. When he's not spending time with his family or writing, he's obsessing over gardening and growing food.

His short story *Darla's Problem* was included in the Splatterpunk Publications anthology *Fighting Back,* which won the Splatterpunk award for best anthology. *The Devoured and the Dead* was nominated for a Splatterpunk award.

He can be found on Facebook, Instagram, and Twitter.

For more about Kristopher Rufty, please visit: www.kristopherrufty.com

For signed copies of books and more, please visit: www.kruftybooks.com

Printed in Great Britain
by Amazon